BABEL

GABRIEL BLACKWELL is the author of *Madeleine E.* (Outpost19, 2016), *The Natural Dissolution of Fleeting-Improvised-Men: The Last Letter of H. P. Lovecraft* (CCM, 2013), *Critique of Pure Reason* (Noemi, 2013), and *Shadow Man: A Biography of Lewis Miles Archer* (CCM, 2012).

BABEL

Gabriel Blackwell

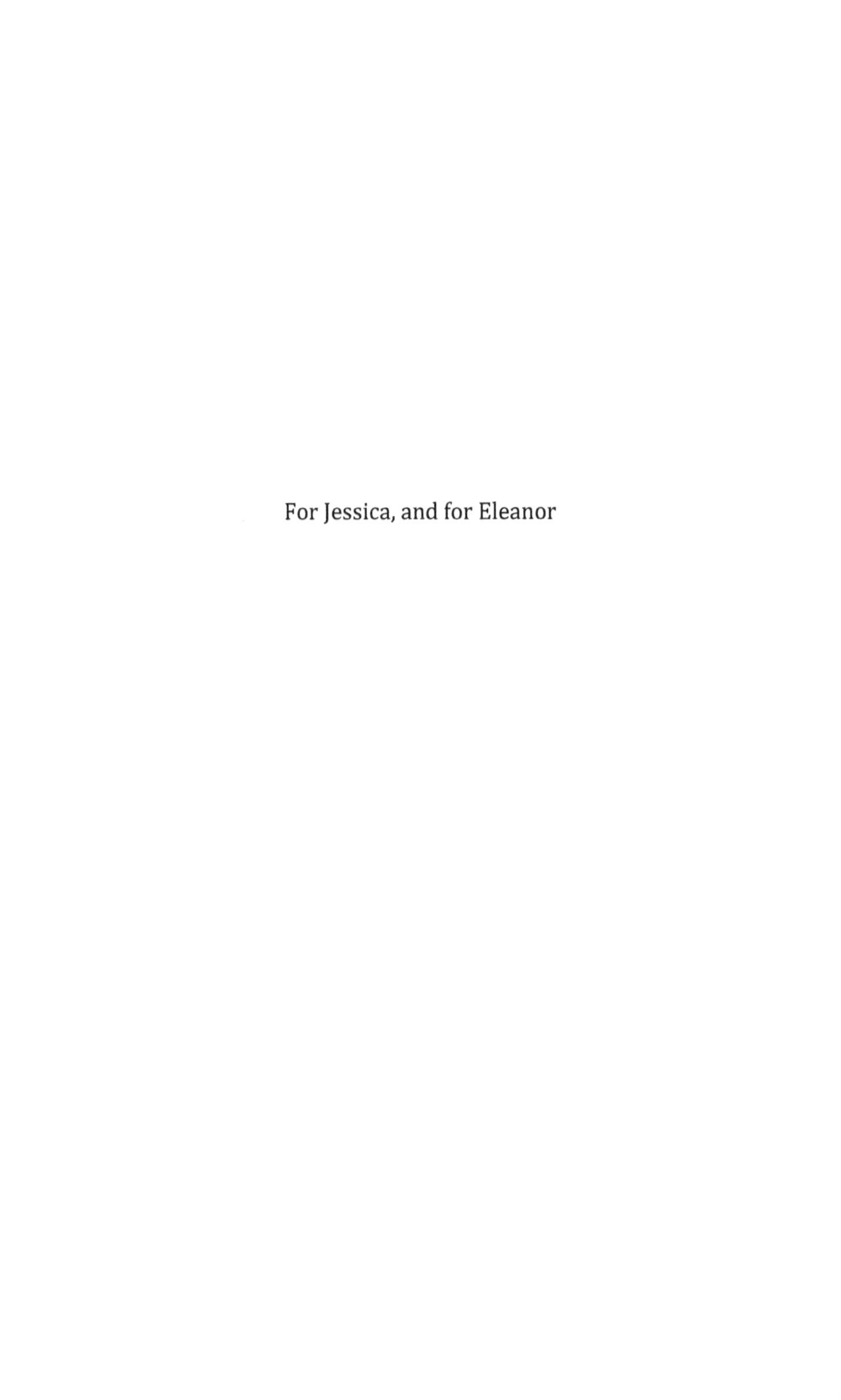
For Jessica, and for Eleanor

Contents

( )

Now alone, knock on Bobby (that most famous of wooden noumena, the not-in-use-just-now dummy of ventriloquist Signor Blitz (known mainly for the spectacle of his opening routine (involving an as-yet-unhandled Bobby firing a pistol at Blitz from across the stage as Blitz enters (the ventriloquist, seeming to exhale cordite, having caught the bullet between his teeth (the trick being that Bobby talks all the while (first, professing anger at his constant manipulation by Blitz, then, once he has pulled the trigger, expressing sorrow at having killed his master (Blitz slumping over on his back opposite Bobby, both thrown backwards by the force of the shot (Antonio Blitz, incidentally, formerly strictly a magician, signature illusion: the bullet catch (given up for the safer profession of ventriloquism when the trick went wrong and tore off the outer lobe of his left ear (leaving him with what could kindly be called an "unfinished" look (proving the man you've just seen to be, actually, not Antonio Blitz at all but an impostor (proving him to be, rather, an American, Clive Robertson (claiming to be the "Original Signor Blitz" (having never seen the original "Signor Blitz," actually a third man whose "true" identity has never been established (officially, as given at admission to Bethlehem State Mental Hospital: "Signor Blitz" (as reported by the *Boston Post* in 1889, twelve years after the second Signor Blitz had passed away in Philadelphia, not from a shooting accident (obituary in the *Philadelphia Register* listing him as Antonio Van Zandt, Englishman (son of a woodworker and amateur astronomer interested particularly in what he called the "ghost moons" of Mars (which would be found, later, to have been real moons, Phobos and Deimos (by Asaph Hall, in 1877, the year the elder Van Zandt's son, Antonio, was laid to rest (having passed away from complications following surgery to remove his gall bladder (which organ was said to have become so diseased that, when the surgeon nicked it with his scalpel, it issued a sound later described as "the knock of a walnut falling upon a wood-beam" (this in the journal of a man so definitively not present at the surgery as to call into question his motives for recording such information (said journalist being also the author of the poem 'Leonainie' (claimed by some to be the "lost" last poem of Edgar Allan Poe (a claim in turn accepted by many others (even elaborated upon—the poem, written after Poe's death, had been "accomplished by another body, but manifested within the same brain," according to no less an eminence than Alfred Russell Wallace (a great debunker of hoaxes, taking on the Flat-Earthers and those who believed in Martian canals (descendants, at least spiritually, of the credulous masses hoodwinked by the Great Moon Hoax perpetrated by Poe's editor, Richard Adams Locke (whom Poe thought had unfairly and without credit scooped out the innards of his 'The Unparalleled Adventure of One Hans Pfall' (leaving the whole thing hollow, in the author's estimation (Poe then creating, in response, the so-called 'Balloon-Hoax,' which asserted much less fantastic fantasies on the part of a Mr. Monck Mason (based upon Mr. Thomas Monck Mason, balloonist, yes, but also theologian and flutist (the flute a woodwind, of course, inspirited wood, hollow and lifeless but producing a distinctive tone when breathed into (

) unlike that produced when knocking on wood only in pitch), immune, impossibly, to charges of being filled with hot air), made mean-spirited through the caprices of public attention), given that his intention had never been to hoodwink, really, merely to entertain), and who now owed Poe a living Poe could never seem to earn through his own labors), who had ascribed the "discoveries" to one Sir John Herschel, a very real astronomer annoyed at having to answer for the bizarreries brought into being by Locke's imagination), as he put it, "creatures willing to credit all but their own credulity"), a man who had become cynical through his powerful yearning to believe, finally, in something, anything)— anything could be believed of Poe!), albeit one that perhaps should have stayed "lost"), a poem whose most memorable lines—"Songs are only sung / here below that they may grieve you— / Tales but told you to deceive you"—are at least fair as *ars poetica*); it would be another fourteen years before a psychologist would review the literature and describe *Pseudologia fantastica* for the first time, and sixty years before Baron Münchhausen's falsifications, amplified by his imitators' tales of him, would become Baron *von* Münchhausen, father to fibbers the world around); the sound also more famously recalling the discovery of a hidden passage, a hollow recess), made necessary, it was rumored, due to Van Zandt's "hollow leg," his high tolerance for alcohol), a year perhaps more significant for the invention of the carbon microphone, a device to electrically reproduce and thereby transport sound), named for a god of fear and a personification of dread, respectively)—a man, incidentally, often said to have been "not all there"), survived by his wife, *neé* Eaton, with whom he had no children), a set of circumstances at least one Massachusetts "Safety Coffin" manufacturer found advantageous, claiming that his expensive precautions had raised Blitz from the dead, or at least had saved him from a costly mistake)—the staff evidently at least somewhat taken in, as the story then leaked to the press); Van Zandt performed as "Blitz, Jr." until he took up ventriloquism and Bobby, renouncing or reversing his false heritage upon becoming a "father"), a claim to originality as obviously empty as it was vehemently made), a man about whom nothing is known prior to his career as the "Original Signor Blitz"; perhaps his "true" identity is just another illusion?), though, given that the existence of these doubles served to multiply the man's fame more than any of his own efforts had, it seems unkind to condemn one and all as "impostors"), like a set of quotations left open), "blank" rounds still capable of propelling anything left in the supposedly-empty barrel at dangerous velocities), utterly unconvincing on stage alone, as though half an act, even before he made himself half an act), the act immediately becoming invisible from the orchestra section), perhaps evidence of this man's great self-loathing, a not-so-hidden threat of suicide), which, it seems to you, is less impressive than his manipulation of the gun, if only because the latter seems so impossible), trials of which had resulted in a gap in the ventriloquist's smile even though no projectile was ever fired)—the gasp this produced sounded as though all of the air had been sucked out of the room through a straw), which, being the opening, gives the rest of the routine a superfluous air, as if the best has come and gone before the act has fairly begun), empty and somewhat deflated, possibly also, you now realize, an impostor): reassure yourself that there is no longer anything there aside from the briefest of echoes, the sharp rap of knuckles on wood and an emptied out double of that sound, signifying that whatever had given this dummy, Blitz's "son," the appearance of life has departed.

The Invention
of an Island

AT THREE OR THREE-THIRTY or, I don't know, sometime in the very early morning around then, my wife woke me to tell me we needed a change. (Or maybe she said *she* needed a change? I don't remember.) She'd decided to install mirrors on all of our walls, ceilings, and floors. She didn't put it quite this way, I think—it doesn't sound like her—but that's as close as I'll get now. Not yet fully awake, I told her we'd have to be extra careful. Extra careful? When she asked why, what did I mean, extra careful?, I couldn't answer. Why exactly did we need to be extra careful? I had no idea. I didn't even remember the conversation the next morning. Why did I feel so sleepy? What was it that kept me up the night before? I must have been napping when she ordered the mirrors. I remember thinking, just before I lay on the sofa: I hope I wasn't supposed to pick up the boy from school.

Often he asked questions, the boy. It was one way I could tell he was my son. To be perfectly honest, buddy, I'd say to him, I don't know what happened to the creatures on Dr. Moreau's island at the end. (This is something my wife would have handled better, telling him that the story isn't really about the creatures, and I'm not saying she wouldn't be right.) He can be a bad influence on me. I'd lose a day's work wondering, What did happen to them? Were they destroyed? Prendick just leaves them there, I think. Were they sterile or maybe sexually incompatible (a conversation I'm not yet willing to have with my son)? Was that something Wells put in the book, or is it something I've invented, this issue of sterility? If they weren't destroyed and weren't sterile, could they—or their descendants—still be there, on that island? My wife, I think, would say that this is nothing to get hung up on; she is, so often, the voice of reason. (I tend to get wrapped up in my son's games and inventions.) It's just a story, she'd say. It's a book. Real life gives us enough to worry about already. But think about the second- and third-generation hybrids, honey, the sloth-vixen-wolf-women and the puma-hawk-monkey-men. In the book, the animal-men return to their original states, sort of, but would their descendants? Would their descendants even be able to, or would they be so far removed from both their ancestors and from what Moreau had wanted them to become that there would be no dry land to swim for, metaphorically speaking? Can that be how the first *Homo sapiens* felt? It's worth thinking about, I think. No, it isn't, she'd tell me if she were here. I have a million other things to do. Don't you?

And now I think I remember that Moreau's creatures did produce offspring (for some reason I'm remembering them as maybe resembling newborn rats? kind of unformed and pinkish and slimy and gross?) but that maybe *they* were sterile? Like mules are sterile? A big part of the reason I have trouble remembering certain things is that my books are gone and I have no way of getting to them. I say this so you understand that if I get something very basic wrong, something that would be a matter of just opening a book and checking a few words, it's not because I'm lazy. Besides, as I see it, it's always a question of my story versus "the story." Really. I've had some time to think this over. See, the story isn't as important as what we remember of the story. Claiming otherwise is kind of like claiming that the fact that an orange has this much vitamin C means that the person who eats it will experience the benefits of exactly that much vitamin C.

That isn't the case. Each person absorbs as much as he or she can at a given moment, and that's what stays with them. It's Plato's cave, I think. (It is, right? Plato's cave?) Again, I don't have the book here in front of me to check, but I'm pretty sure that what Plato is saying is that there *is* a figure behind the shadow thrown on the cave wall, it's just that we never see that figure, we only see the shadow.

I tried a version of this argument out on my wife a few days ago. She didn't buy it, but I hadn't completely thought it through then, so that's understandable. We'd been discussing the boy, I think—we usually were, although lately she had wanted to talk about the book instead—and she brought up something I'd once said that she thought contradicted what I was saying then and accused me of playing devil's advocate. (Actually, I think what she said was something more like: You always think I'm wrong, which isn't true, but for me to have said so would have contradicted what I was trying to say. She's so smart!) I told her that if I couldn't remember what I'd said, that I probably didn't mean it— I mean, that's basically what I said. I don't remember exactly what words I used; something along those lines. But as I said, it doesn't really matter, and anyway she didn't buy it.

Now, though, I could tell her about Plato. I could tell her about the cave and the shadow. The shadow is kind of like a Rorschach blot, if you think about it. You can interpret it however you want and you won't necessarily be wrong. But the thing throwing that shadow, it's only like itself, it only has one way of seeming. (Or, wait, maybe that's inconsistent? I want to say that Plato would say we interpret only the shadow, not the thing throwing it—that that thing is a kind of absolute or essence—but then I wonder if the shadow is already that interpretation and I feel like I'm in over my head with this metaphor.) I could tell her about the orange. I could tell her: For instance, honey, the thing that probably a lot

of readers miss in that book I was telling you about, Bioy Casares'
The Invention of Morel, is that the people on the island are also
the missing passengers of a freighter later discovered adrift. The
book doesn't spend that much time on that part of the story, but
it seems really significant to me. What could have happened to
them? The crew of the freighter is found dead, without hair, without nails on their fingers or toes, their corneas dead, their skin
dead. (I remember those details perfectly, though honestly I'm
not sure why Bioy Casares bothers to include them, since he goes
on to say that these people are dead, which would seem to cover
just about everything being dead, skin and corneas included. But
anyway.) The boat doesn't make any sense if it has no passengers—
what would it be doing out there?—but there is no mention of
passengers in the book. At least, that's what I remember. So,
anyway, another boat discovers this ghost ship, sinks it, and then
tells everyone back at port that the island it came from is now
cursed. We're led to believe that it's Morel's invention that has
done this to the crew of the ghost ship, and that, because the crew
was exposed to his invention for significantly less time than the
people on the island, the people who should have been aboard
the ship, that those people must have dissolved or disintegrated
even further than the crew has, until they finally disappeared,
which is why they aren't on the boat at the time of its sinking.
Could this maybe have to do with the invention's true purpose?
Not to record these people but actually to immortalize or transform them in some way? What if what happened to them just
looked like death to everyone else?

I could tell my wife all of that. She might not listen, but I could
tell her. I could say: Whether or not it's part of Bioy Casares' story,
it's part of mine. The shadow's all we've got. If it isn't actually in
the book, that just means I get something different from his story
than he did. But that's natural. It's like quantum physics, like how

you can't measure something without affecting the measurement. Which, I think, means that you can't really measure something, you can only measure your effect on it. But wait. I'm getting off track. About the mirrors: she had read an article that said that mirrors made a room look bigger. We lived in a cramped apartment, which—no, I shouldn't say it—well, okay: the boy's stuff was everywhere, and what made it worse was that these were things he never used, things we'd been told were necessary for one reason or another, by books, television, teachers, and other parents. My wife, too, had her craft nook and the better part of the living room, while I managed with a desk in the hall closet. She said, I think, that she was curious about what a mirror facing a mirror would look like. As I recall it, my feeling—which would seem to have stayed with me despite the fact that I couldn't really remember the conversation during which it was formed— was that we maybe shouldn't find out. But mirrors were installed anyway. I was famous in our home for being averse to new things, and so usually changes were made despite my protests. (Which, in my defense, weren't exactly protests, but more like lines of questioning.) When the boy changed schools, for instance, I was the only one wondering if it was the best course of action. My wife has never particularly cared for this aspect of my character, and the boy has recently begun to question it, too, which is part of the reason I indulge his fantasies—to keep him on my side. What about our son? I asked the night after the mirrors had been installed, talking in my sleep (not unusual); also, I guess, seeking answers in my sleep (very unusual). The next morning, before she too disappeared, my wife relayed this information to me and answered my question: We have no son. And she was right. He had already disappeared. But all that was after the mirrors.

I'D LIKE TO THINK THAT, rather than being intractable (as I'm sometimes accused of being), it's just that I want to think things through before getting into them (natural, I'd say, for a person who writes about his life as much as I do), and there's always a lot of thinking to do. I will admit that this sometimes involves a Zeno's arrow of patience on the part of others. Sometimes my wife would rather just shoot the damn arrow, and who can blame her? Work had begun in the apartment before I was even awake from my nap. If the movers hadn't bumped into the sofa while carrying my desk out, I might have awoken hours later, in the moving van, still on the sofa. I didn't understand where my wife could have borrowed the money to pay for it all; paying for our son's school was already a challenge, given what we made. (Well, to be fair, what *she* made. My writing brought in very little.) But it was done in an afternoon, our home newly resplendent. The mirrors, however, made it extraordinarily difficult to navigate our apartment. Though I had some familiarity with the layout—I mean, we'd lived there for seven years, ever since the boy was born—I still found myself lost, and completely so, not just turned around or momentarily confused. It happened almost immediately after the mirrors' covers were taken off. Even the act of walking across the room was a significant challenge, as it was nearly impossible to judge distance, and the boundaries of the room seemed to change with one's position. And there was the issue of my reflection getting in the way, repeating enough to make me unsure as to whether I was approaching or stepping back from whatever was in front of me. I'm sorry if that seems confusing; it was confusing for me. Basically, every step meant that one of my reflections got bigger and the rest of my reflections (of which there were many) got smaller, except that in getting smaller, they were multiplying and so also, in some way, getting bigger. It's impossible to convey in words. It almost made me nauseous, the sight of it. Think motion sickness.

The people who'd installed all this had had to remove the furniture and everything else in order to do so, so all that was left was one enormous, room-shaped mirror. If I'd had my wits about me, I would have asked my wife why she thought this was a good thing, but, well, I didn't have my wits about me, and anyway we were both tired from the commotion of having had the mirrors installed. We were so tired (and, frankly, so lost and confused) that we simply lay down on the mirrors and fell asleep. We wouldn't have been able to find the bedroom, and there was no bed in it anyway. When I awoke (no idea what time it was, all the clocks had been removed) we had the conversation I've already mentioned, and then at some point (again, no clocks) my wife was gone. I don't know if she'd followed our son into a mirror (an absurd thought, but one that occurs to me) or whether she'd left by the door (an equally absurd thought, for where now was the door? *was* there a door?). I really can't say—it was difficult to tell, even when she was there, which her was *her* and which was her reflection. I don't know. You know, I'm not sure I'd even slept next to her, or whether it was she who had answered my question about our son. Which seems like a ridiculous thing to say—a reflection obviously can't answer a question—but you know what I mean. In any case, whether or not she had found it, I couldn't follow her because *I* could no longer find the door. I wandered from place to place (unless, as I now suspect, I didn't, I simply stayed in the same place, going in circles) until finally the dizziness was too much. It felt like I was in an elevator whose cord had been cut and whose emergency brakes only worked when I closed my eyes. I sat down. I think I slept. When I stood up and stretched my legs later, I noticed a line of smudges on the mirror where I'd just been laying, an outline of my body (or at least the warmer and maybe grimier parts of it) that looked like some kind of semi-transparent archipelago. Or what's the one when it's just a ring? An atoll?

It occurs to me that I may be giving the impression I sleep a lot. I mean, here I've said I woke up, napped, and then, a few hours later, fell asleep again, and then, even after waking up, fell asleep once more. But that's not quite right. I think—and perhaps a psychiatrist or neuroscientist could say for sure—that this might have to do with the fact that I mostly sleep now, now that the mirrors are here, and maybe memories work like dreams? So that they kind of project back to you what you've experienced most recently? I do sleep a lot now (although without a clock and without any clear indication of time passing, it's really impossible to say) but I haven't always. Because of the dizziness I've already mentioned, I spend a lot of my time with my eyes closed, and it's kind of difficult to stay awake when your eyes are closed for hours on end. *You* try it. Unfortunately, this leads to a lot of headaches and just aches in general—I'm not used to sleeping this much, and the mirror isn't terribly comfortable. But what else am I going to do? I either have to sleep or hold my head very, very still, focusing on that line of smudges, since everything else here just reflects back and forth and makes me sick.

They seem more defined to me, the smudges, more defined and maybe a little more filled in, too, maybe just by virtue of the time I've spent lying here. I don't want to come across as gross, but I think what they really are are dead skin and follicles and sweat and grease. They are, right? So what I've called my archipelago is really kind of almost like a corpse, in a weird way. Maybe that's a morbid thing to say. Somehow, though, thinking that way makes me feel oddly like Prendick preparing to leave Moreau's island. As I recall it, Prendick does a kind of Robinson Crusoe in reverse just before he leaves, salvaging what he can from the island to outfit a boat, making another island out of the boat. Like Prendick, I've packed those things most essential to my survival and left the rest behind. (Montgomery, of course, smashes the boat to splinters before Prendick can use it, though Prendick does eventually get off the island. I think he also builds a raft? But then the raft falls apart before he can get it to the water? Hmmm. Now I wonder how he *did* get off the island. There's no Montgomery here to smash up my boat, but maybe that's because my Montgomery's already been through, with the people who did the mirrors.) As for Morel and his friends, they don't even have to worry about how they'll get off their island—they're rescued by the boat I've already talked about, though whether they reach their destination seems doubtful. I guess I mean that in the traditional way, not in like a metaphysical, Lacan's letter kind of way— they reach some destination, obviously. I must be waiting for my rescue boat, since I have nothing to make a raft out of. (*Do I?*) I *can* make waves, just by turning my head, but it remains to be seen if there's any way of crossing them.

This is a little off-topic, I guess, but I think Morel gets off light, especially if you compare him to Moreau, who, say what you want, but at least Moreau experimented on animals and not people. I mean, Morel informs everybody of his reason for asking them to the island (*aide-mémoire*: he wanted to record them using the titular invention, a new kind of recording that, when played back, would reproduce not only sight and sound but also touch and even smell (Wait. Smell?)), and tells them what the effects of his invention on others have been. (Unless that was another character who told them about Morel's friend suddenly falling terribly ill and then dying? I don't remember now.) I think a few people get upset, but nobody really confronts him, at least not from what I remember. He just kind of runs off in a huff because they don't give him a standing ovation for killing them. Probably even then, on the island, some of them are already feeling the effects of their exposure. I mean, yes, there is no indication of that in the projected version of events witnessed by the refugee who narrates the book, but suppose that the invention worked partly by leeching more of the essence of a person as time went by, so that, even as the subject's corneas and skin die, the corneas and skin of the projection grow more and more real. Doesn't that seem likely? Maybe I'm overstating myself. Doesn't that seem possible? It would have made for better recordings, since, as the people being recorded got sicker, their recorded selves would have gotten better, become more substantial. I'm thinking particularly of the wall that the refugee smashes open in the basement: when the projection is running, the hole he has opened is not only closed, it is impenetrable, but when the projection isn't running, he can smash through thick concrete with a stick or whatever he uses. Not to mention, it would obey the laws of thermodynamics. (That's what I mean, right? The whole thing about matter neither created nor destroyed? I mean energy, I guess, but I think energy and matter are reflections of each other? Isn't that what Einstein's theorem is all about?) But I have trouble understanding why Morel would do this to himself, why he was sacrificing not only others' lives but his own—and for something that he would never himself enjoy. Unless he knows something we don't. If I had been there, I would have spoken up in that meeting. It's not unusual for me to speak up. Wait. Is it unusual? I feel conflicted all of a sudden, I can't remember a time when I did speak up like that. But I feel like I would have been the one to cut through all the passion and emotion others were displaying at that moment. (Though I suspect that if I had, my wife would have said, Well, there he goes again— never wants to try anything new. I'm not saying she'd be wrong.)

I wouldn't dream of blaming Wells for the arguments my wife and I have had lately. That would be ridiculous. (I may as well blame the mirrors, or the boy.) But my son and I were talking it through, *The Island of Dr. Moreau*, hunched over a model I'd made of the island and the seas around it (he was using some of his action figures as creatures, I think, and explaining to me what animal each one was) when my wife arrived home from work. This was a few days ago. First she praised the boy (was this for school? she asked) and then, when he told her it was mine (he's a humble boy, and honest), she grabbed his arm—rather roughly, I thought—and took him to his room. I could hear her voice through the walls, though I couldn't tell what she was saying. I'm sure it was something reassuring, but I remember thinking that her tone would have frightened me, if I had been in his place.

My son's fascination with *The Island of Dr. Moreau* was what was to be expected of a boy his age, I think. He liked to imagine what the animal-men looked like, what they *were* like. Wells, too, was probably interested in these animal-men; I get the feeling they gave him his reasons for writing the book. But it also seems to me that regardless of why Wells wrote the book or what interested him in his premise, he nonetheless tells a more compelling story along the way: that of Moreau, isolating himself from something he loved in order to—well, I'm still not sure what. Maybe it's telling that this is what I think of when I think of the book? I don't know. The scientific community has cast out Moreau for what they considered to be offenses against morality, and no matter what discovery he subsequently makes, it will be condemned as yet another of his enormities. (It kind of seems like there's justification for this, given the nature of his experiments.) Why even bother, then, to continue as a scientist? Wouldn't it be better simply to give up, to enter another profession? He could open a pub, or go into bookkeeping, I don't know. Is it better—for the creator, I mean, for his or her soul—to create something that he loves but with which experts in the field find fault (or even turpitude) or to create something for which he has no passion but which the experts find satisfactory? (My wife might have asked, with good reason, whether the reviews of my latest book made me wonder this, but I don't think they have anything to do with it. Reading *The Island of Dr. Moreau* to my son really affected me. I had to stop because I didn't want to cry in front of him.) Is it better to feel unhappy with what one is doing but to be accepted as part of a group doing that thing, or is it better to feel unhappy because one is pursuing what one wants to pursue but is alone in doing so?

I know, I know, I'm getting side-tracked again. I was talking about my wife. Or the mirrors? Maybe the boy. Let's start with my wife. So, as I remember it, after she'd put the boy to bed, she reminded me that our son was already doing poorly in school: he was often distracted and tended to ask questions that his teachers felt indicated he wasn't developing normally. Their advice: a therapist, possibly drugs. I wasn't in favor of this, but, well, as my wife would say, No surprise there. During parent-teacher conferences earlier in the week, my wife asked the teacher what she thought normal development looked like. The teacher explained about degrees of curiosity and avoidance and sort of implied, I think, that perhaps something at home was the source of the problem. When it was my turn to pose a question, I asked about the drawing on the wall, a big drawing on butcher paper, clearly made by the teacher's students. She informed me that it had been made by her students. I said, Yes, but what is it of? What's happening in the corner down there? Are those waves, and maybe a raft or something? My wife gave me the same stern look the teacher did, and then they continued their discussion without me. When we got home, I put the boy to bed with the first few chapters of *The Island of Dr. Moreau*. I think it was the drawing that had made me think of the book, but now I can't be sure. Maybe it was something my wife had said? I can't remember. Anyway, when he was asleep, my wife told me she had finished reading my book a few days ago—this is what I think I remember—and maybe had been trying to talk to me about it since then? I'm pretty sure she said she felt I hadn't been fair to her, unless I think she said that because I think now that maybe I actually haven't been fair to her. Anyway, I'm pretty sure I said something about criticism as a creative act, and I'm pretty sure she didn't really take it the way it was intended. She said something about using this imaginary son as a wedge (I mean, how could I forget that?) and then rolled over and went to sleep. I stayed up a little longer, reading *The Invention of Morel*, which reading *The Island of Dr. Moreau* had reminded me of, for obvious reasons.

You know, now that I think of it, maybe the reason Morel secludes himself on the island isn't because he's worried about his friends' reactions to his explanation of his invention, but because he's already beginning to show signs of the invention's effects. After all, he would have been the one to have had the most exposure to it. He says he's recording everything because he wants this happy time to go on forever, but really, he's rarely part of it. Instead, he hides in his room—isn't that a little suspicious? Even in his room, he's part of the recording, the invention is exerting its effects upon him. Maybe he would have been visibly sick even before everyone gets to the island. Was he wearing a wig and make-up when he met them at the launch? Gloves? If you had just watched your friend die an awful death because of something you suspect you yourself may be suffering from, what do you think you would do? Would you become afraid of infecting others, even if you knew that "infection" was impossible? Wouldn't you try to somehow get away from them? It must have been terrifying. Maybe Morel's friends don't scream at him because they pity him.

But here I am again, talking about something that's not even in the book. (Unless it is?)

I remember once telling my wife about the feeling I had about finishing some book, it might as well have been *The Invention of Morel*—I felt somehow more lonely, as though my entire group of friends had all suddenly moved away together, or as though, completely unprepared, I'd been taken out of my home and set down in the middle of nowhere. Maybe it's a stretch, but couldn't that be how Moreau felt? On his island, having shut the book on London, on science? Or did I actually tell her that? Maybe I just thought it but didn't say it. Maybe I'm thinking it now but didn't think it then. I think she said something like, It's fine to think about these things when you have time, but there are also lots of things we *have* to do in order to have that time to do that kind of thinking. She would have been right in saying something like that, but I worry that I'm not being fair to her in attributing that thought and those words to her. What if the wife I'm remembering isn't my wife? I guess what I mean is: what if what I remember is just a really small slice of the life we actually lived together, and I'm forgetting all the things that made me want to live that life? Or what if I was the one who thought that, who said that, and she just agreed? What would it mean if I remember her this way but she was, in fact, in life, some other way entirely? Was she much kinder? Was I much crueller?

At first, when I realized my wife had gone, I called out repeatedly, my wife's name and my son's name. At least, that's what I remember doing. But the strange thing is—and you can try this if you don't believe me—the strange thing is that when you say something over and over, it starts to lose its meaning. Maybe even worse, when you say something over and over and it starts to lose its meaning, you start to doubt whether it's even what you mean to say, especially when it doesn't have the desired effect. I haven't used my wife's name here because I don't really know what it is anymore, or I don't know that I know anymore. At one time, I think, I thought I knew, but now I think I don't. But I don't know—I might be misremembering that I once knew her name. I can't say. I've lost my son's name, too, and I've started to doubt my stories about him, and if you think that isn't a tough thing to handle, well, it is. When I think of the things I think I know, I'm now more conscious than ever that that person thinking those things isn't me, is only more or less like me, like the me I see in the mirror, except in my mind. See, if I sit perfectly still and look straight ahead, I can open my eyes without feeling dizzy, so that's usually what I'm doing when I have my eyes open. What this means, though, is that I'm looking straight into my own eyes, and this has become, by now, disconcerting. (Is that what I mean? Yes, I think that's what I mean: disconcerting.) Because, I think now, maybe, partly, because those eyes belong to a past me, not the me whose eyes look into them. It is a past me; it must be, right? Because light travels at the speed of light but still isn't instantaneous? So the me I'm seeing is a person that doesn't exist anymore. In a way, this makes perfect sense, since the same thing can't occupy more than one space (if it does, it's two things, one that occupies one space, and one that occupies the other)—so, for me to be able to see myself, I must be looking at another thing which is not myself—but it must also mean that what we think we know about ourselves isn't so. Our brains work even slower than light moves—I mean, light is the fastest thing there is, right? We can't know ourselves, in other words, we can only know what we think of ourselves, which is really another person entirely thinking those things, the person we think of when we think of ourselves. Maybe I'm making too much of this, but sitting in a room lined with mirrors will do that to you.

I almost never dream here, but last night (actually, just last time I slept—I have no idea if it's night or day) I did. In my dream, in a room I couldn't get to—which could be any room, since I can't seem to leave this one—maybe by whatever process light makes its way to me here in this room, I saw my wife and son leaving through what looked a lot like our front door. (How *does* light get in? The only thing I can come up with is that maybe it was let in before the final mirror was installed, and now it just bounces from one surface to another, endlessly. Is that possible? It's probably not, but I really couldn't say, and, anyway, it's all I can come up with. On the other hand, if it *is* possible, I'm not sure how my wife and son would have gotten out without also letting out this light. (Is *that* possible? Can light, which is both a wave and a particle (right?), leak like water or sand?) And I'm not sure what it means if my wife and son would then have disappeared, leaving no traces in these reflections. And then I have to remind myself that it was a dream. It was a dream, right?) I wanted to call out, but I had forgotten their names (which, as far as it goes, is as real as anything else here, so maybe it wasn't a dream). Nothing at all came out of my mouth. I stood up, and the room shifted as it always does, and I felt my stomach drop, and I staggered toward where I had just seen the door. It seemed to be getting smaller, so I turned around, thinking I had just been deceived by the mirrors, but in every direction that place where I thought the door had been was receding and fading from memory. Was it in that direction? Or that one? Now that I can look left to see right, or look down to see up, does it matter?

I IMAGINE MOREL ON THE BOAT. Somehow he has survived a good bit of exposure to his invention, exposure that starts long before everyone else gets to the island—his friend, the doctor or professor or whoever, dies, but he, Morel, doesn't. Maybe he's immune to the invention's effects; maybe he just knows better how to stay out of its way. Now, like soap under water, his friends have dissipated. The members of the crew have looked on in terror. They put all the sickening, disintegrating people in the hold (meanwhile, on the island, the projection gets better and better—what had been wraithlike and nearly transparent is now opaque, almost solid) but the infection spread before they could isolate them all, and now they, the crew, feel weaker, less like themselves. Theirs is the feeling of being spread thin, of being so busy that one feels as though one has tried to be in two places at once. There were grumblings about Morel from the infected passengers when they first came aboard, but, since Morel was the boss, the crew turned a deaf ear to the rumors. Now, though, the rumors can't be ignored. The first seaman's nails blacken and then fall off. He didn't look good a few days ago, but now his skin is turning gray. The other men lock Morel in his state room. Morel says nothing; he hasn't said a word to anyone since he boarded. He paces, mostly. Because they have been so sick, none of the sailors has bothered to go down to check on their quarantined passengers, not for days. When one of the men realizes this, he sends in another man. That man goes, returns, and reports that there is no-one there. On the island, a woman's nervous laughter breaks the silence, and then the silence returns. Somewhere, though, someone is crying. A seabird on its way north swoops down out of the sky to eat a piece of bread left on a table beside the pool, but it can't even move the bread, much less eat it. A ghost ship looms off the coastline of the island. The waves look oddly like the outlines of sailors busying themselves anchoring this ghost ship, but the whole thing disappears when cloud occludes the sun. Another bird flies down and snatches the bread out of the first bird's beak. The first bird complains and flaps its wings. The other bird ignores it. On the boat, the seamen open Morel's cabin. They want an explanation.

Why isn't he getting sick like everyone else? Does he have a cure? He barely even looks at them; better, he looks through them. Finally, one man shoves Morel. Perhaps it is that the man is so feeble that he cannot budge Morel, who still seems to be in good health. Though it has had no effect on Morel, the sailor's act of violence gives the other men permission to act as well. A second man throws a punch, cries out at the impact, then shakes his hand in pain as if he has just punched the bow. He has broken bones. Perhaps it is due to the movement of the clouds, but the ghost ship off Morel's island flickers again, just a bit. Another man kicks Morel, but, he, too, cries out and immediately recoils in pain. He sits down, hard, on the deck. The first bird flies after the thief, into the trees. The thief throws back its head, and a bit of bread disappears. The first bird is calling, getting closer, but the palm fronds won't make way for it as they've just done for the thief. The bird hits them—they are as solid as the trunk—and falls to the ground. Someone has the idea to get one of the rifles. The man takes aim at Morel. The noise of the gunshot in the ship's corridor is awful. The bullet, crumpled from the impact, falls to the floor and slides, wobbling, to the base of the small desk in the corner of the room. The sailors lock the door again. Morel stands near the desk, perhaps mumbling something about the island, the invention. The boat drifts. Most of the sailors die on the same day, within minutes of each other, sparing them at least that horror. Morel, in his cabin, continues to pace. The men from the Japanese ship (I'm almost certain it was Japanese) come aboard and discover the bodies of the sailors. They are curious about the locked cabin, but they can't find the key, and nothing they say or do produces a response from inside. Given the gruesome state of the bodies they've found, the Japanese leave the boat as soon as possible and decide to sink it despite one sailor's contention that he saw a man still alive and seemingly in good health, pacing, in the locked cabin. When they ask the sailor how he could have seen into the locked cabin, he replies that, for a brief moment, it was as though the bulkhead was transparent. Actually, in that moment, he says, the whole ship was transparent. This man—the man who would have been in the cabin if there had been, in that moment, a cabin to be in—was suspended in air in the trough of the water produced by the (momentarily) invisible boat. It was, the sailor says, as if he had parted the waves. It was as if he alone on Earth knew some secret.

Fathers and Sons

I did not find my father at home when I returned. My sister said he was gone. I think we must have played in her room until dinner was ready. I do not remember what we ate that night.

I READ THESE LINES IN THE LETTER and wonder: can one write about the disappearance of a father the way one would write about stamp collecting—I mean when it's someone else who has done the collecting—about butterflies, birds, I don't know, sports, coins, cars, Precious Moments, any of those incomprehensible passions other people seem to possess, trivia, in other words? The answer, I suppose, is yes.

And, look, before we go any further, please understand, I am a miserable person and I know it. My good fortune has never seemed particularly good to me. I have, on an embarrassing number of occasions, only just barely stopped myself from complaining about the problems my wife and I have with our son to someone who, for all I know, can't have kids, or lost one young. There are those who have it worse, I mean, and, in my better moments, I recognize that my way of seeing the world is cowardly and childish and to be regretted. And there is also the convenient deafness I tend to develop when my daughter demands my attention, and the reproach I see in my son's face when I tell him I love him—though of course I know there is no reproach there, not really—and then there is also my tendency to make things about me when, in fact, they aren't.

My trip to the library was a duty, then, an obligation I felt I owed my father. It was my father who'd written the letter, about *his* father, my grandfather, and I guess I couldn't stand to see my father's words seem uncaring by comparison. I needed, I mean, to compare. I did not want my father to be alone. So I trailed along behind the librarian, not dawdling exactly, not drawing things out, only being careful not to get too close to this woman, a woman who, frankly, to me, seemed to cultivate the distance I was keeping through both her bearing and her attitude, a woman appearing, at first, physically frail but carrying herself as though she possessed a wild strength—a woman, that is, depressingly familiar in her affect, but also, it seemed, a sincerely helpful and solicitous person, even if very possibly incapable of showing it, handing me any number of books, mysteries, yes, thrillers, true crime, all books dealing with the sudden disappearances of both men and women, handing me book after book so that the pile rose to my chin, and then, finally, a book clad in plain binding on which I could not find a title, saying, *This one may interest you*, her strange, possibly unintentional emphasis on the word you and the lack of a title on the book somehow together sparking a memory in me, a memory from two or three years earlier, when I'd been in another library, this time with my son, handing him impossibly thick books, books without illustrations, all of them about birds, thinking perhaps this will be the one that finally bores him as much as the whole subject bores me, perhaps this one will cure him— and I knew, even then, that I was being ridiculous, insensitive, insulting, stupid—cure him, that is, of his fascination, his obsession, so that, for once, he and I could have a normal conversation, one in which both of us participated and responded to each other, one in which I did not feel as though I was interviewing him for

Birding Enthusiasts Monthly, one I wouldn't complain about later, in bed, to my wife, so that, turning out the light with a heavy sigh, she wouldn't look at me as though she were seeing someone she didn't recognize and say, *Would it kill you to take an interest? He's reaching out, as much as he can.* I glanced again at the books the librarian had handed me and I thought, surely, if I looked close enough, in each one there would be some near-explanation of, or partial excuse for, my father's tone, some hidden wrinkle to his story. Then I thought of the weight of these books in my hands and the flat affect of the librarian and I worried that I was really only corralling yet more facts, crowding out the finer feelings I'd most hoped to uncover, and so, saddened, I could think only of leaving the library. As soon as the librarian had passed out of my line of sight, I left the books on the cart I found at the end of the aisle and slunk away, knowing, as the books slid out of my hands, that the librarian would later find this stack, arranged in the reverse order she'd handed the books to me, on the cart, and in that moment she would know that, though she'd done her best, I had nonetheless failed to follow through, failed to uphold my end of the bargain, failed to so much as consider her efforts. She would know, in other words, that I was quite simply not a serious person, not someone to be trusted. Perhaps, like my son, she would shield herself further from those who did not share her enthusiasms by immersing herself even more deeply in those enthusiasms. Perhaps she would be as bewildered as he was to find that common ground had shrunk, become scarcer, in the process. Who cared for her? Who listened patiently?

I'm not likely to come off well, I know, but I still feel as though I should say my actions were not, whatever they might seem, the result of some wanton cruelty. I had already read quite a few stories of disappearances, including even one or two of those the librarian had handed me. I knew the general tenor, I'm saying.

That wasn't my problem. While its effects had been hidden from me at the time, this reading had, in the end, succeeded only in making me more anxious: here were stories, above all, of men and women for whom life had simply become too much, though often this part of the story was buried beneath the testimony of those who'd known them. *He seemed so happy*, they wrote. *Life was good. He had so much to look forward to.* Yes, all had appeared to be perfectly normal to everyone around these people, much as my own life did to me before I'd begun reading. But then, inexplicably, they'd gone missing. Questions inevitably arose. Had there been secret debts? A second family? A fatal diagnosis? Perhaps it was only among families of the missing, but it really started to seem as though every man, woman, and child harbored the same exact suspicion: that there had to be something someone out there was not telling them. One Saturday not long ago, my wife told me, apropos of nothing, *You know he loves you*, and I immediately thought, to my great shame, *Why is she telling me this? Did he do something I don't know about? Will I hear something from his aide on Monday?* I was, I mean, not exempt. Far from it.

MY FATHER'S NAME, my father had written, *is or was Rudolph Fentz.* See? Only the first line and already I had a question: why that *is or was*? Really, though, I had many questions. I had, first of all, no idea why my father was writing this to me. I hadn't known Rudolph Fentz, had been born much too late to have met him, hadn't even known his story. I had, as a child, often been compared to him, especially in terms of temperament, and I felt then that these comparisons must be unfavorable, though perhaps they only seemed unfavorable because he was a man I'd never met—the comparisons came off as if I were being judged to be unknown, even unknowable, a phantasm, something one could not say was definitively one thing or another, good or bad, liked or merely tolerated. Then again, maybe my father saw something in me, some dormant, suspect gene he had unwittingly passed on and of which he was, in his own way, trying to warn me.

In any case, most of what I knew of my grandfather came by way of these comparisons. To go by what my father said, I shared not only my grandfather's features but also some of his mannerisms, his inscrutability, his uncertain bearing, his nervous energy. Was my father, in those moments, willing me to display some atavistic relationship to his father? Is the saying really that the son is the father of the man, or is that just some Freudian trick my mind is playing on me? Not that my father ever treated me as his father, but it did seem, in reading the letter, as though I were reading a story that was making obscure promises to reveal some further, unseen aspect of our relationship.

And despite the letter's ostensible subject, it doesn't have much to say about Rudolph Fentz. My father sticks to the facts, and because there are so few facts about his father's disappearance, the letter is short, only two pages, handwritten, front and back. Somehow the letter's thinness makes it seem as though Rudolph Fentz was merely one of many fathers who disappeared during my father's childhood. My father's feelings are concentrated in this one line, a *non sequitur*: *I remember I did not like it when he kissed me because his beard scratched my skin.* That single sentence made me realize that, in relating only the events that occurred rather than how he felt about them, my father was actually avoiding the story he'd set out to tell. I did not know whether he knew this.

Although I had a beard when my son was born, I have since shaved it. I can remember my son fussing and crying after I'd kissed him on the top of his head, the look of radiant anger he'd get seemingly any time I came near, my wife's palpable frustration when she'd finally put him down. The first few times, I figured it was just me and felt embarrassed but, with repetition, my embarrassment was replaced by a dull kind of anger.

BECAUSE, I SUPPOSE, my father had been hospitalized when my grandfather disappeared, and because he'd been terribly ill even before that, there is nothing to be found where one might expect a matter-of-fact report on my grandfather's last hours at home. My father did not, could not, know what those hours were like, and perhaps it didn't occur to him to wonder, so in place of describing them he wrote a brief paragraph on what was known of his illness at the time. It seemed there were many misconceptions going around then—misconceptions about, most perniciously, the severity and spread of his disease, but also about its causes and its prognoses. Rudolph Fentz in particular had apparently been warned that, because of certain personal risk factors beyond his control, he was not only susceptible to my father's disease but even likely to develop water on the brain and swelling of the heart should he contract it. He had therefore been counseled to stay far away from my father's hospital ward, far away from the hospital itself.

This enforced distance could only have been a torment for him. It hardly seems necessary to say that his son, my father, was terribly sick, in fact on the verge of death, and Ingrid Fentz, Rudolph's wife, my grandmother, was at the hospital around the clock. She slept on a rickety steel cot the staff brought in for her and ate only on the rare occasions when some nurse remembered to put an extra plate on the tray. She would later say she felt sorry for Rudolph Fentz—it was his *son* he couldn't see, after all—but at the time she must also have felt deeply angry with him for not visiting, not helping out, and, because she'd barely slept and eaten, her nerves must have been frazzled.

Now, it's true I've made up some of these details, maybe even most of them, but please understand I did it only because it seemed necessary. No-one else is going to bother. In one of the books the librarian had handed me, one I'd read before, the author, a war widow, wrote that she was horrified by the last thing she remembered saying to her missing son—he was half the man his father had been, something along those lines—but then also wrote that she'd said this at least a day before he'd gone missing. She'd been over their last twenty-four hours together dozens of times with the police, but somehow she couldn't remember a single word she'd said to her son after this thing she regretted, and yet, she wrote, she *had* to have spoken to him again. Were her real last words to him *I'll get that* or *Maybe so*? Final moments with the missing were, in the books I'd read, almost always part of the mystery, but, aside from this one aside in this woman's book, their significance went unacknowledged. Anyway, it's basically clear from the letter's subtext that Ingrid and Rudolph fought over who ought to be at the hospital, that one of them must have been there to look after their son, my father, and that that person definitely wasn't Rudolph Fentz.

One imagines Ingrid, worried, thinking about what she'll need to take to the hospital with her, knowing she won't be able to leave until she is given the all-clear, discussing things with Fentz in their tiny apartment. Their infant daughter, my aunt, is in the next room, screaming. *Why haven't you fed her yet?* Ingrid asks Fentz. *I've been talking to doctors all day, going from this office to that one, and where were you? Do you really care so little for this family you can't spare a moment to feed your daughter?* Maybe this is too much; maybe, I mean, I am overcorrecting for my father's lack of emotion. Ingrid, turning from the counter, brandishes a knife, and Fentz scampers from the kitchen. *Coward!* Ingrid says. She had merely been making a sandwich to take with her—

who knows whether they'll feed her? Only a coward, she thinks, a coward like her husband, would have seen the knife in her hand, the tone in her voice, as a threat. And anyway, what kind of person would you have to be to think that she, Ingrid, a mother so devoted she was putting her life in danger just to be there with her son, would do such a thing? This person who had promised *in sickness and in health* was no help at all. Did he think the whole thing would go away if he didn't look at it? Was he afraid of their son? Was he afraid of her? She heard what she thought was Fentz rifling through the closet for something—a bag? a coat? nothing was missing from the apartment when later they checked—and then saying, in a voice muffled by the closed door, *I'm going to see my son*. That was the last anyone ever saw or heard of Rudolph Fentz.

MY SON, the boy who, at the end of daycare, used to grab the squat polka-dotted bolted-down tables and refuse to let go just so he could keep playing with the white-and-blue stuffed bird he'd already been with all day—Zazu, maybe?—wrestling with his aide while his mother or I waited nervously outside for the two of them to appear at the door, would want me to say that this illness my father had was later found to be genetic, and so the fears of contagion he describes were completely unfounded. My son would, if disappearances were birds, tell me that 76%—a number I've made up; no doubt my son would know the correct number if missing persons were his passion—that is, a sizable proportion of all disappearances, are really something more like the resistance he put up at daycare, I mean men and women who, obstinately, do not want to appear, do not want to be forced to go on with their day. And he would want me to say, furthermore, that the police do not officially consider a person to be missing until several days have passed for a very simple reason, because, if they suspected they had a murder on their hands rather than a missing persons case, those days they insisted must pass before they could begin their missing persons investigation would instead be considered absolutely crucial, *so* crucial, in fact, that those same police would tell you there is only the slimmest chance of solving such a case, say 13%—again, my son, no doubt, would have the number on the tip of his tongue—if no evidence turns up during that time, and that the case would then be called "cold," so that the reason the police don't consider someone missing until several days have passed has at least something to do with the fact that they know those missing people would really prefer not to be found, and so it's only polite to just leave them be.

But then my son would not tell you any of that, because none of it involves birds and he really only cares for birds. When the sun has gone down and there is barely a glow around us at the edge of the grocery store parking lot—where, it should be said, we'd gone only to get the hot dogs my wife, at home, is waiting for; *Take him*, she'd said, obviously tired, and I'd relented mostly out of guilt—and I try to take the binoculars from my son's hands and he holds on so tight I can see his muscles tense even in the semi-darkness, and I almost feel I can hear the scream I know is coming, and I look around to gauge just how many people are going to see me smuggle him into the car, thinking I'm a pervert, or a bad dad, or who knows, and when I'm sitting behind the wheel, finally, holding the package of hot dogs to my eye and feeling it soothe the rising bruise, when I've almost but not quite swallowed my frustration and am able to speak in a relatively calm voice, telling my son it's all right, my eye will be better in no time, I love him no matter what, I'll look over and notice he has turned on the dome light so he can scan his Audubon, and I'll want to say, *You know, it's also possible that Rudolph Fentz went to the hospital only for no-one to remember seeing him there.* But my son will have no idea what I'm talking about, so we'll both sit there in the car, staring straight ahead, him at his book, and me at the road.

Given how short my father's letter is, it would seem ridiculous to drag this out any further; I've already written twice as much as he did. So let me come to the end and tell you about the strangest part of his letter, the part I've puzzled over the most and the part that ultimately set me to writing this. My father, though he often seemed quite taciturn to me growing up, is a feeling person, a man of sensitivities. Maybe it's that he has melted over the years, softened, or maybe I have. Though he never—not once—brought up the subject, still he could not but have felt the loss of his own father acutely and for nearly the whole of his life. Just the fact of it seems enough to excuse his silence. And yet, despite this, despite what I know or at least must hope is there, somewhere, in his heart, at the end of the letter, just where it would seem excusable, even appropriate, for sentiment finally to creep in, perhaps anger or self-pity, there are instead two fairly long paragraphs on the subject of conscription. The history of it, I mean, not his feelings on it. Given what's there, I think it's much too generous to say he was trying to imply his father had been drafted or shanghaied, somehow pressed into service, on the way to see his son in hospital. It's improbable, anyway, and there is no such connection drawn in the letter. There are just these two paragraphs on conscription, presented without context, as though my father had forgotten which letter he was writing. Did someone out there have a letter with all the emotion missing from the one I'd received? Some history lesson that suddenly swerved into absence and loss? I think probably it's too much to hope for.

Perhaps, then, to make up for this strange and disturbing lacuna in my father's letter, I should tell you my own feelings about this thing I am myself now writing, this thing you are reading. It is, of course, imperfect in almost every aspect, as anything is—there are too many abstractions at the beginning, it doesn't get rolling until page two, and so on—but then maybe, I'd like to think, it only seems that way because of my own unreasonable ambitions and expectations for it. I would like to say that it is something of which I feel proud, even if only in the most thrilling moments of its creation, before I had a chance to look it over and compare it to my fantasies for it, before I'd found it wanting and then slowly, agonizingly slowly, realized it was really only *me* that was wanting, *me* that was disappointing. Does the frustration come from the fact that I've finally put into words this suspicion I've had for so long, that whatever there is in me is corrupt, and so whatever comes out of me will be corrupt as well? I look over the top of the laptop at my wife trying to hurry our son through his morning rituals so she can drop his sister off at daycare and still get to work on time, and then, later, at my phone as I sit in the car, waiting to work up the courage to face my son's aide after yet another fight at school, and I wonder about those long-ago comparisons my father made. How was I like Rudolph Fentz? Was there time to change? Was there really the will to? Perhaps it's better to write about birds, I think, or conscription. Just the facts.

La tortue or
The Tortoise

DECADES AGO—in fact only a few months after I was born, though of course thousands of miles away and as thoroughly unrelated to my birth as a butterfly's stretched wings to a distant hurricane—the French publisher Gallimard brought out a collection of texts attributed to Jorge Luis Borges called *La tortue* or *The Tortoise*. At least according to the book's description, none of its essays, fictions, or "unclassifiable prose" (the translation is mine, I should say, as are any mistakes in it or in any of the translations that follow) appear in Borges' *Obras completas*, and thus their discovery—in French translation, no less!—ought naturally to have been an event. The book's fate was, however, otherwise. *La tortue* was printed but never distributed, its publisher or its editor perhaps having had a change of heart regarding its authenticity. There are no court documents to rely on now; there is no documentation of any kind. There are rumors, naturally, but the rumors are of recent origin and so less reliable. Copies are said to exist, for example, unread and unsold, in a warehouse in a suburb of Paterson, New Jersey, and why a French edition of an obscure work said to be by an Argentinian writer would remain unread and unsold in an un-named New Jersey township is, it seems to me, completely under-standable, but why such books would have come to be there in the first place is considerably more of a mystery. My efforts to locate the exact site of the warehouse have so far come to nothing.

In an essay whose title I haven't been able to find, appearing on page 175 of *La tortue* and (once) accessible via Google Books, Borges writes: "It is a species of melancholy to have to do with books that have met with such a fate." The page this quote appears on is the only page of this particular essay to make it into Google's preview. Most of the page is devoted to an enumeration of the various editions of the Bible and the degree to which the apocryphal gospels are integrated into them, yet the Bible isn't the subject of the sentence. What fate is Borges speaking of? Which books? I don't suppose I have to say why I found this particular passage so intriguing.

There are fifteen pages total in Google's preview of *La tortue*, but no ordering or library holding information, no ebook offerings, and seemingly no way to know how Google's scanner got his or her hands on the thing. Nor is there any information about why the book was assembled in the first place—the more important question, it seems to me. According to the pages I was able to access, *La tortue* includes, among other things, a review of the book *Unwitnessed Spectacles, 1890-1900*, a book that doesn't seem to exist but which apparently details such phenomena as the washing up of two mermaids in advanced stages of decay on North Avenue Beach, Chicago, the opening and subsequent closing of a sinkhole one hundred yards across in Jordan, and Marconi's transmission, from the SS *St. Paul*, of the entire text of de Quincey's *Suspiria de Profundis*. *La tortue* also includes a list of untranslatable texts (eg., the schizophrenic A.A. Barnes' English-rendered-phonetically-into-French *À qu'il lise*) along with a commentary on the proper construction of temporary structures meant to collapse, like those in Buster Keaton's *Steamboat Bill, Jr.* and Jean Epstein's *La chute de la maison Usher.* There are at least 256 pages in the volume, as the last page that appears in the preview is numbered 255 and the last sentence there reads "Of all the books I have sent to press, none is more personal than this motley, disorganized"—obviously concluding on the following page, ending mid-thought as it does.

I probably don't need to remind you that Google's preview function doesn't allow the reader to control which selection is chosen, and that that selection may change over time. For example, at the time of this writing, I cannot check whether what I have transcribed above is accurate, as page 255 is no longer part of my preview. I have re-checked the preview often over the past month, hoping to be able to read more of the text, but the same fifteen pages show up each time—and these, again, are not the same as they were when I first discovered the book and began writing this essay. Given the empirical evidence, then, I must conclude that if I were to check the preview every day for the rest of my life I would see the same fifteen pages, but if I were to leave the thing alone and only check it, say, once more, on the day I died, perhaps I would see a further fifteen pages, having thus read, over my lifetime, only a fifth of *La tortue*. Granted, my knowledge of the inner workings and algorithms of Google Books is non-existent.

Just a moment ago, my wife called to me from downstairs. *Honey,* she said, *the children are waiting.* They will all be arranged around the dinner table, a plain pine table chosen for its simplicity and now scarred at its ankles by the dog's incessant chewing, two sets of hungry eyes centered above matching Donald Duck plates and my wife's eyes, urgent, tired from her long day of caring for the children—all of them, that is, except for the youngest, who will be set back a bit in his high-chair, a bib around his neck and a Diego sippy cup affixed to his hand (unless he has thrown it, the cup, I mean, to get my wife's attention). They will wait for me to be seated before eating, a rule my wife invented, that we all be together before the meal starts; they will even wait long after the dishes have been set down steaming in the middle of the table. In my imagination, they will wait forever, though I know this isn't so, and I wonder at my fantasized cruelty. Who am I, even to myself? If the food gets cold, they will complain of course and my wife will be upset with me, but still, I think, they *will* wait (again, except for the youngest, who has already eaten). I will get up from my desk, piled high with books I will never read, and I will cross my office to the recently-oiled-but-still-creaking door, just barely cracked so that I can be called to dinner but mostly closed so the children will know not to bother me, and I will open the door and I will walk down the hall to the top of the stairs and I will take hold of the banister, loose and runneled from the children sliding down it, and I will descend the thirteen steps to the first floor, and I will cross the hall to the kitchen, passing the dining room to get the salt shaker or the pepper grinder or the water jug, or any other forgotten thing, and I will ask my wife and children, from my place in the kitchen, if there is anything anyone needs, and then, finally, I will enter the dining room and my children will smile or look at their plates, depending on how long it has taken me to do all these things, and then I will sit and I will tell them about Borges' lost book, or anyway the book attributed to Borges but which may not exist and may not have been written by Borges, but first, first I will have to command certain muscles to extend and other muscles to contract so that I may rise from my desk, which any-how is covered in old, yellowed bills and empty envelopes, not books, and before I can do that, I must have the impulse to rise, which, just now, is too much to ask, I think, for I have been hungry for days and have had very little to eat, and, perhaps more im-portantly for this essay, I must have a desk to rise from, a desk and a chair, and I must have work that demands time at that desk, and so I must have some sort of education, perhaps some sort of experience, in order to get such work, and before I forget, I must also have a wife, and children, and so I cannot begin because at present only some of these things have been accomplished and not even necessarily the most important, such as the children, who exist only in my imagination, since, before one can have children, one must have a kind of hope, and my wife and I have instead, in its place, debts, for I am a mostly-unemployable scholar and she is employed by a temporary agency as a file clerk, and we are neither one of us in good health, and so we have not started the family we ought to have long ago started, "long ago" because I am nearing middle age and she is not far behind, and we live, childless, in an apartment that is much too cold and too small even for the two of us, and completely unsuitable for children, and this is a source of much friction between us, and we spend the nights we ought to spend dreaming together each on our own side of the bed, lying awake with our separate worries, hers more serious than mine owing to certain health problems making pregnancy a complicated and even dangerous proposition but mine still strong enough to wake me at four in the morning when there is absolutely nothing else to do but think about what has yet to be done, how much further there is to go, how little time there is left—for any of us, really, but for the two of us most of all.

The Student

THE YOUNG MEN the man's wife brought home were all very young, eighteen or nineteen. They were, he knew, students enrolled in his wife's classes. Now that she had voluntarily terminated her leave, she went in even on weekends, or at least she left the house.

The man's wife never bothered to hide the fact that she was taking these young men upstairs and fucking them. After an interval of thumping and groans, the man would hear the shower running and then there would again be quiet in the house. Because he now slept on the floor in the spare room, he wouldn't see his wife until she left the next morning. He never saw any of the young men leave. He worried they might even now somehow all be upstairs, dozens of them crammed in up there, perfectly still, making no noise. He imagined the cracks in the plaster spreading across the spare room's walls were the result of all that weight.

In some ways, the man thought, it was his wife's brazenness that made it so difficult to confront her. She had absolutely no shame about this thing she was doing, and so he had nothing with which to appeal to her better nature. Really, though, it was that his wife was never in the same room with him long enough for him to have made an appeal. She was out of the house, or on her way out of the house, or else she was upstairs with one of her young men. She knew, he suspected, that he had become afraid to go upstairs.

THE MAN WAS PART-OWNER of a shop that sold tabletop games. He was in charge of the strategy section. After his wife started bringing young men home, though, the man did not go in to work. One of his partners texted. Why weren't they open? Had the little one arrived? Congrats if so! The man didn't respond.

Instead, he put the clothes in the drawers in the spare room into boxes. In the drawers, they'd been arranged by article of clothing—socks together, pants together, onesies, PJs together—but in the boxes he arranged them all according to age: three months, six months, three to six months, newborn. He took the crib apart but left the mattress on the floor and brought the boxes and the crib down to the basement. To make room on the shelves, he got rid of some of the backstock he'd brought home from the store, stand-ups and dice and maps for games he would never play. The only thing he didn't immediately toss was a box of un-painted miniatures from some role-playing game he didn't recog-nize and the book of scenarios that went with them. He couldn't understand why he'd brought these things home.

There were two Cultists in the box, both wearing the same baggy, vaguely exotic clothes. One had a large veined mass or tumor bulging from its stomach, with a tail or worm hanging off its lump that came to a sharp point like a spear. The other had tentacles jutting out of its face where its mouth ought to have been and, above them, a beak instead of a nose.

A third figure, the Doctor, was the only miniature clearly de-picted in the illustration on the box—though there were Cultists in the background in a strange pyramid-like formation, their only identifiable feature was their baggy clothing—and the fourth miniature didn't appear anywhere the man could see. The Doctor stood at the center of the illustration in the foreground, a long, thin blade in his left hand. The knife was missing from the miniature.

The fourth miniature was apparently called the Student, though the man couldn't see any reason for giving it that name. The Student wore no clothes and looked like an infant but enlarged. It was as if someone had held a flame too close to a plastic mold of the figure of a baby and then, when the mold had melted a little, stretched it to give it the proportions of an adult. There were blisters or buboes all over the Student's skin.

A rough stone altar or table appeared at the bottom of the image on the box, on the right, mostly cropped out on the front but continuing onto the side. At first glance it looked as though this image might have wrapped around to the back, too, but when the man turned the box over, expecting to see the Student or the two Cultists or all three, the back was instead a bright white with a plain cardboard border. Or no, not quite—there was the faint shadow of what looked like a face impressed in the white near the bottom left. Its features made it appear to be upside-down. Maybe some ink had transferred from the book the box had lain on? The man turned the box back over. Looming above the Cultists was an immense monster he hadn't seen at first because it was the same bright white as the back of the box. It looked almost like a production error. Cultists dropped from its mouth or else were being sucked up into it. Really, the most impressive thing about the illustration was the shading in the sky between the humanoid figures and the monster above them. It suggested, somehow, an infinity of other possible creatures.

ARE YOU—are you here for my wife? he asked the young man at the door. Anything he could have said in this situation would have seemed absurd. This was the first time one of her young men had come to the door on his own—they'd always arrived with his wife before, usually after dinner. Possibly as a result, the man felt flustered. This young man was wearing scrubs, and this was unusual.

She's not here, the man said. She's at her office. Do you have the number?

The young man waited where he was outside without in any way acknowledging the man's words. The man debated what he ought to do. He couldn't simply close the door, but he could find nothing further to say. He stepped back a little from the door and turned, as if to indicate to the young man that whatever he wanted wasn't here. The man's wife, who he was certain was still at work, was somehow home instead, standing on the bottom step, perfectly silent. There was something about the way she looked in the light that seemed foreign to the man. She'd put a wave in her hair—normally, she wore it straight—and he did not recognize any of the clothes she had on.

Eventually she said something, but it was something he couldn't hear, as if she was speaking in another house and he was looking in at her through a closed window. The woman's husband felt a fluttering at his ears, like at a change in air pressure.

The young man in scrubs passed in front of the man, carefully closing the door behind him. He joined the man's wife at the other end of the room. The two disappeared up the stairs.

The next morning, something very strange happened.

Instead of leaving for work as she always did now, the woman stopped somewhere behind her husband. He could feel her staring at him sitting at the breakfast table staring at the book in front of him. Coffee, he said. He motioned to the French press, almost full. He should not have felt ashamed, but he felt ashamed. He could not look up or meet her eyes.

According to the book, in *The Student*, players are enrolled in a class on cults and charismatic leaders, with a particular focus on a local moon cult led by a mysterious figure named the Doctor. Whether the Doctor is a medical doctor or an academic, and thus how the players ultimately come into contact with the Doctor, is left up to the game master. The end of the campaign depends on what the players uncover during the course of their research—

certain interviews and documents may, for example, reveal that the moon cult's sacrifices are, unwittingly, summoning a horrible phantasm from a distant star, or that the cult is engaged in fertility rites intended to result in the birth of something called the moon dæmon, or that, through a kind of mass hypnosis, the cult has taken over the town and intends to turn its resources to raising a moon fragment whose impact is said to have created the nearby dry lake. Players who die don't simply exit the game or roll a new character. Instead, they are reborn as antagonists who attack and feed on the other players. In this way, there are no losers, or there are only losers. The man was more used to the zero-sum games of his own shelves and displays at the store.

What was very strange about this was that the woman also didn't say anything. She didn't sit down at the table.

I think, her husband said. It's just, her husband said. When he looked behind him, she was not there.

THE YOUNG MAN who showed up that night looked very tired, almost drugged. Maybe, the woman's husband thought, he *was* drugged. Like the last one, he wore scrubs, but this young man's scrubs had fading maroon stains across their front.

I don't think she's here, the woman's husband told the young man. Is she here?

The young man's lips moved, but the woman's husband didn't hear anything. He leaned in closer.

The young man smelled like rubbing alcohol or some sort of cleaning agent. The husband also caught a whiff of burnt toast. In that moment, it was very hard to think. He had the sensation that the invisible force that held him to the floor and the floor to the joists and all of it to the ground had lost its grip, and now he and everything around him except for the young man was slipping upwards, into the atmosphere and beyond, completely unmoored and out of control, into the emptiness of space. The feeling made him dizzy. The woman's husband reached out and grabbed the doorframe to keep himself from floating away.

Behind him, the woman had appeared. The young man's palm pressed gently on her husband's chest. The feeling was cold and piercing and instead of feeling it where he'd been touched, her husband felt it just above his left eye. He released his grip on the doorframe and, with the crazy thought he'd lost contact with the earth beneath him and was headed for the ceiling, crashed awkwardly and heavily backwards onto the floor. The young man stepped over the woman's husband and followed the woman upstairs.

The woman's husband would have called out if he'd been able to, but instead he only lay on the floor and tried to orient himself. For a moment, it had felt as if he hadn't been there, like he'd been put under for surgery. The moon shone in through the still open door. His eyes could not adjust to its brightness. Blinded, the woman's husband used the hall table to pull himself up. The lamp next to the bowl of keys crashed to the floor and there was a popping sound as the bulb broke. Upstairs there was the usual noise.

Each time before he'd felt without reason that what was happening upstairs was none of his business. What had happened had been tough on both of them, he thought. He hadn't handled it well and she hadn't handled it well. She deserved time to figure it out. But the real reason he hadn't done anything was simply that he didn't feel up to the demands of the situation and very badly wanted it to resolve itself without his involvement. Wouldn't she get tired of this eventually? Possibly she'd just run out of students. He was not religious, but many nights, curled up on the tiny mattress in the spare room, he'd found himself praying to a higher power to come down and offer some kind of relief.

This time, though, the woman's husband heard a sound that was not the sound of the woman or of her young man: the cry of a child so much louder than the other sounds up there but then suddenly choked off.

The husband stumbled upstairs. His feet felt heavy and he was exhausted and couldn't draw a full breath. His eyes were half-shut. He banged on the door of the bedroom he'd formerly shared with the woman. There was no answer. He heard the shower going, so he turned the knob. The door wasn't locked and somehow this made the woman's husband feel ashamed—he could have done this, he thought, at any time, on any one of the previous occasions, and only his own cowardice had ever prevented it. What if he'd done this the first night she'd gone upstairs with one of the young men? What if things had never reached this point at all? He was terrified of what he'd find on the other side of the door.

In the bedroom there was the strong smell of smoke and sulfur. The woman's husband hadn't been upstairs since before the woman first brought over one of her lovers. Not only when she and her young men were here but also not when they were not. He'd used the bathroom on the first floor, slept in the spare room. And yet everything was where he remembered it, his water glass on his side of the bed, half-full, and his old pair of glasses sitting on top of a book he hadn't finished. The bassinet next to her side of the bed. The stuffed sea creature in the corner of the bassinet.

There was no young man. The woman's husband thought he must be in the bathroom with the woman, but it was strange that the young man's scrubs were not there on the floor. The sheets on the bed were messy with some slick, dark liquid, and in the center of the bed was a very still infant about the size of the woman's husband's closed fist. Tiny, very tiny, and not moving, not breathing. It was purple with creamy white vernix covering most of its face and one of its legs. One of its arms was much longer than the other, the length of its entire body, and one of its eyes was open, staring straight at the woman's husband but without consciousness, without life.

WHEN THE WOMAN came out of the bathroom, she screamed and her towel dropped to the floor, and instinctively she shrank to cover herself. The stranger on the bed was hunched over something. It looked like he'd had an accident, she thought—the bed she'd made was pulled apart and streaked with a thick brownish substance, and in the center there was a small figure, a carving or statue she was too distracted to identify.

Get out! Get out! the woman screamed. Get out! She couldn't help herself—the words just came up out of her chest and through her mouth. She was shaking and screaming uncontrollably and she didn't know what to do.

The woman had already run back into the bathroom and slammed the door and turned the little fin on the knob to lock it. Now she retreated as far into the room as she could, into the shower. She pulled another towel around herself, closed the frosted door, and mentally scanned the room for any kind of clothing or protective gear she could put on, anything she could wield. Ever since she'd seen signs there had been someone else in the house—weeks ago now—she carried the can of pepper spray up to her bedroom at night. It would be there on the nightstand where she'd left it, she thought.

There had been a man, an ex, who her friend called *the stiff*. A month after they broke up, she'd awakened one night to find him standing there above her. Even though it was too dark to make out his face, she'd known it was the stiff as soon as she opened her eyes—she'd caught him watching her sleep a couple of times when they'd been together. It had been one of many reasons she couldn't wait to be done with him. When he saw she was awake, he left on his own. That was typical of him—he didn't do well with conflict, tended to freeze up any time they fought, which was often, because he was also controlling. His sudden appearance that night had been scary. She couldn't quite bring herself to believe he wasn't hiding somewhere in the apartment even after she checked every room, every closet. She'd changed the locks and her routine, switched shifts at the clinic. When she could, she moved.

The police officer who answered her call about the things missing from the basement and the sweat-stained mattress she'd found on the floor of the spare room had asked her over and over if she was sure she hadn't cleaned out the basement herself, if she'd had visitors, a maid service, anyone, a neighbor, possibly, who might have had keys to the house? She told him about the stiff. She looked into getting a restraining order.

I'll call the police, she said. Get out!

She didn't have her phone with her—it was plugged in on the nightstand next to the pepper spray—but the stranger might not know that. I have a gun.

The stranger mumbled something on the other side of the door, sounds the woman couldn't identify as any language with which she was familiar. It sounded like crying.

The woman screamed. She couldn't make herself calm down or quiet, but through the noise she was making and the trembling of her body, she realized that the stranger was saying the same thing over and over again. It wasn't quite chanting—he sped up and slowed down without any obvious pattern or rhythm—but she could tell he was repeating himself. Then there was silence. Then there was the muffled sound of something heavy dropping onto the carpet.

The woman was saying Please please please. Oh God, please please. She pulled herself up out of the shower, and, hesitating, placed her hand on the doorknob. She listened. The light in the room seemed to brighten until it hurt her eyes. The dull ache she experienced was deep, somewhere under her forehead, the feeling left after she'd rubbed her eyelids with her fists too hard.

She turned the knob. She remembered a moment that couldn't possibly have happened: the pain of the head crowning, the pang of fear at the quiet that followed, a man at her side she didn't recognize, weeping. The warmth of a light shining in her face and the cool that spread over her after she moved into its shadow. She was doing so good, this man was saying. So good. Everything was going to be okay. She was doing good. What was that snaking out of her? Back in the bedroom, a pit had opened in her stomach, a feeling like falling.

A Field in Winter

BEFORE, in the bathroom, I'd lapped at the last of my brother, mixed in I guess with blood from the trucker. The haunting-space it would show me would be like looking through the surface of a lake: what I saw there would be displaced, and so, clumsied, I would be unable to grasp things there as I might here and vice-versa. But it wasn't that I wanted to hold anything or bring it back; what I wanted was to avoid the visit altogether, get in and get out, and this seemed the best way to convince father to ignore me—to visit him twice. First I would go as my best self, my ghost, the one he could grab only in memory, then I'd go again later, in reality, as though still a ghost, liberating my brothers from their guardian.

In order to appear there I had to picture him as he was, bring him into focus, but the environment around me kept intruding. The arc lights and the gas pumps and the passing cars shone through my thinning perception. I had been looking in on what was elsewhere for so long that I seemed to have weakened my hold on what was in front of me, and I doubt the dilution did me any favors. They tell you to imagine a house when you want to remember something. I wanted now to remember a house and its inhabitant. You put a thing in a room and another thing in another, and through that you walk, in your mind, until you have the whole. It had never worked for me, but in my desperation I tried it again.

In the mudroom, beside the door, was a dark stain, not mine, in the shape of a brother. It might have *been* a brother; it might have been an oil stain in the parking lot or a stain I had once

observed at that spot in the mudroom—I don't know—but whatever it was, it would have to serve to help me rebuild the house.
In the kitchen the sink had been ripped out of its cabinet and now
lay on the floor. Something scurried behind me, a rat or a person
or worse. When I turned around I realized I'd only *intended* a sink;
I worried, in looking again, that the silhouette I saw might instead
be the trucker, or something else. Was I overthinking things? Or
underthinking them? None of the rooms were lit, as though my
mind, in seeking to be faithful to my memories, was instead vetting
them. Like shapes in the dark, my perception of the things in these
rooms changed even when the things did not.

In the dining room was another stain, a smear, and some sort
of open bag. A set of footprints led me further into the house.
Through the archway of the living room I saw a blur, the only
thing alive in this haunting. And by *alive*, I mean *in motion*. It was
my father but sped up, moving five times quicker than he ever had
in life. I went upstairs after him. In the first bedroom, the closet
was open and my mother was half-inside, bleeding from somewhere near her center. She wasn't real. Though she had been gone
longer even than I, she was as essential to my memory of the place
as the fanlight above the door or the knob on the banister. In the
second bedroom—my room, though my father never respected
the distinction—the wall had been papered in pages from some
almanac. The back bedroom held only a brother, cradled in his
bottle of spirits, bobbing slightly on his stiff legs. I went downstairs, into the light. In the front room a notebook lay open, with
writing on the page, and in the bathroom there was a button-
down shirt, soiled and draped over the lip of the sink. My father
had been wherever I would be before me, and now appeared
behind me in the doorway of the bathroom. I turned to face him
and he hurried down into the cellar. In the cellar, there were bot-
tles of spirits on every counter, wooden planters lining the floor,

and a heap of composted brothers next to the furnace giving off their own heat. The smell was such that I retreated through the cellar door, out into the field.

I'd done it wrong, I thought. This was a method of memorizing, not one of remembering or envisioning. I'd walked through and saved that sequence of things in memory, but in doing so I'd only brought those things and myself out into the field behind the house. The last seven months, I'd pretended my father didn't exist, and now I was undoing him even in memory.

WE DROVE PAST THE EXIT and into the sunken landscape surrounding the city. I said, We passed the exit, thinking the trucker hadn't seen. He didn't even slow down. Did I forget to say that this was before this story started? It was, a thing that happened that existed before this became this story. Not so far back as my exile, but back far enough. There could have been a different story, is what I'm saying. But then the trucker had drunk from my brother's bottle, and he'd driven past the exit, and gradually this story became this story.

He'd had a look of purpose about him, the trucker, a serious-ness that reminded me of my father, but maybe it was only in each case an abatement of violence.

No, I said, you don't understand.

He'd thought the bottle held an invigorating agent, or at least so it seemed from the way he'd swigged it. He also had a knife. After, he looked like he'd swallowed a wasp. When he finally open-ed his mouth, it wasn't to speak but to spray the windshield with a slime thick with blood, and to then slump over onto the steer-ing wheel. It was clear he'd had too much. Wherever he was, he wasn't here. Each slanting minute took us another mile. I started counting, one mississippi, two mississippi, but I only got to fifteen or twenty.

I don't think I thought my brother had taken me somewhere, I only knew I was there and then I wasn't. I was in a field behind my father's house, a different one, one like the surface of the moon. I used to dig holes there, I remember, and my brother was with me in my memory or my dream or whatever this was I was in, in that field, whole, unfettered, even on two feet and, one supposed, ambulatory.

I remembered I had gone to this field every day after school until father caught me and asked me to quit. He didn't like me using his tools. I'd ruined some of them, it seemed, because of how I was made. Our mother had been barren, hadn't she? People said I was a miracle, but they didn't know a thing. Sometimes I found bones when I dug in the field, but usually they were small bones, easily mistaken for almost any tuber. They would always be soaking in small reservoirs of ruddy liquid; sometimes the liquid would shoot out of the ground when I cracked the clay around them, imparting a tingling sensation on the skin not to be confused with the burning that accompanied any imbibing. Once I had come home gory, and father had cried a little and said, Your brothers. Don't disturb them. He didn't talk much, so I'd learned to heed his words. This time, though, in my dream, my brother and I disobeyed. We were pelted. The field around us, I saw, was cratered with unhealed holes. I guess, in the dream, we'd been looking for a while.

When I realized where I really was, I was in the ditch next to the truck stop. There was blood on my shirt and in my hair, just a bit, and my brother was missing, as was the trucker.

My father kept a journal: yet another thing, I remembered, that my mother had been suspicious of. It was, as far as I can recall, just a lot of nonsense about growing things out of season, and proper watering, and the reproductive properties of certain soils, even the right breed of dog, mixed in with bits of conversations he'd had months after the fact. I couldn't understand a word. I don't know how he kept track of what was what, but he was good at pretending it all mattered. I remember it had required quiet. So much of father had revolved around silence.

I thought about this journal the way one rehearses what one will say before one says it. I was readying myself. I didn't yet know I would find what was left of my brother but still fail to haunt our father as I'd known it to be done, suffering this present confusion. Since he'd mostly lost his hearing, father had refused to communicate with people, though he always went through the motions just to be rid of company. He'd nod or shake his head, depending on the facial expression of the person talking, and would even sometimes add a *Yeah* or a *Huh* when he saw the other person had stopped speaking. None of what was said made any difference to him; he went on as though it hadn't happened. There weren't any visitors since the screaming started. The few people in town he had to see on his errands got his book, and conversation, such as it was, happened on the page when it had to happen. But this was an uncomfortable method for conversing, and it led to certain awkwardnesses, and people didn't like it. When it came to emotion or deeper understanding, everything had to be inferred:

> *Isaac is gone and these this year all unripe. The sound of the last*
> *drew attention from the crows.*

A little less faded, and in a different hand:

> *A black whelp? Why? What happened to yr dogs, Abraham? No,*
> *they wouldn't. What of?*

My father replied often enough aloud. He couldn't hear well, but he could still speak. I assume he did so on this occasion, closing the book. The rest is in his hand, in other ink:

Maidenhair, ginseng, damiana, rhodiola: effects now limited. Too old for seeding? None thrive. Wednesday—evening sun, humid soil. West wind. Waning crescent. Will it ever again be right?

This was the page I had seen in my haunting.

THE ATTENDANT SAID the man had been in the bathroom for an age. He'd looked rough and smelled, she said, and she'd sensed something wasn't right. She didn't intend to disturb the occupant is what she meant. I had an idea it was the trucker—blood on the pavement outside and in the attendant's description—so I angled the Allen wrench I'd found in a parking spot next to the ice machine in through the doorframe and carefully lifted the latch, scooting it left. The man lay on the ground in the ruins of the trashcan, bloodied napkins soaking up the mess. He was broken, his head cracked open by the sink. My brother had already mostly dissipated, his vessel smashed. I squeezed several napkins out into my mouth, about as much as I thought I would need. I don't know. It failed. I've been over that.

I stumbled away from the parking lot across the country separating me from my father and my brothers, and every few steps, something would come up at me out of the past. Aftereffects, I thought, made strange by the crash or the contamination. The smell of copper and rot that had lived in my father's cellar rose from the untrampled ground in front of me. The moon, slinking out from behind the clouds, was replaced by the memory of my mother's insulted face on the day my father brought home the seedling that was to be the first of my brothers. The black dogs always thronging the house, made nervous by any sound, swerved around me like a school of fish around a rock, and the snapping from beneath my feet became the sound of roots being torn out of soil by dogs straining to reach the meat my father, off in the distance in his protective headgear, held out to them to entice them to pull. My heart responded to the shrieks my memory reminded me were coming. And then there they were, making me cover my ears, and something newly leaking from me, a distant ringing and a change in the atmosphere around my temples like water entering or exiting my head. I fell down from the pain of it.

All of it, everything I thought laying there in the cold furrow, was predicated on my father's fear of being a failure. My birth he celebrated, but my life he had only resented. Where now was his heir? He could not console himself upon my mother enough. The groaning had never stopped until mother scraped herself out with some implement. Then he brought home the seedling. Then mother disappeared. Though no-one thought it distinguished him, my father believed that to be a father would make him something more. To raise crops made him a farmer; to raise men would make him a man above others. But then there was only me. Was it possible we were, all of us, wrong about him? My brothers hadn't lived, no matter what else father did, and they were not really men, as much as they might have looked like them in miniature. The best he could do was bottle them in spirits, keep them preserved until something crept in. Myself, I suppose.

These pickled men, my siblings, appeared to me at school and again while playing at a neighbor's. I tried to introduce them to my playmates, to be polite, but my playmates only ran off shrieking. Their screams startled my brothers, whom I could not reach out to comfort because they were only ghosts, but I remembered I'd wondered why, why these sounds would worry them, sound being central to their nature. I had no answers, for myself or my brothers. In any case, these apparitions had somehow given me the idea of drinking their medium, and that in turn had led to father casting me out when he discovered the trick. I had appeared to him in the field—I have a meager imagination, I admit—and he'd had to cover himself before threatening me. I remembered, too, that I had been afraid until I realized he couldn't reach me, and then, where I lay on the cellar floor, I vomited, hard, and almost choked, and all of it—father, the field—disappeared. He didn't believe in it for some time, and then he did.

And now he hung in the air before me like my brothers once had, swinging just slightly as if to taunt me. I couldn't see too well in the darkness, but his silhouette made him appear almost naked. Because he wasn't touching the ground, I felt sure he couldn't be real, but he looked as though he'd aged, was now different than the man I'd imagined, the man I'd lived with so recently. I went around him, well out of his reach. He didn't lunge at me or make a noise, but I would swear his eyes were open. I don't know; it was still dark, but there had been that flash. When I searched the house, it was as empty as it had been in my vision, and I couldn't now be sure whether I wasn't in fact just haunting it. Was I seeing something already over? Was I still at the truck stop, in the truck, on the road, in Mr. Strick's pavilion? I wandered through the rooms. No furniture, just soil in piles and swells like sand dunes, or, at certain moments, nothing at all. I quickly grew confused, since the things of my vision weren't really there, or, rather, I wasn't there to touch them. There were things there, I just couldn't see them properly.

When I turned the corner into the living room, father slipped into the hall. In order to avoid him, I went upstairs, but he had preceded me and was coming down. The sight of him in that darkened house made me cry out. He couldn't hear me, so it didn't matter, but I had my pride. I scuttled out of sight into the cellar. He had preceded me there, too, and hung from a rafter by his belt, over the planters, in the altogether. Because his weight had twisted him around, he'd managed to miss the planter—his seed, I could see, had dried on the hardpack floor—and the brother underneath him had withered and died. I had the presence of mind to grab the only brother left, open and mostly consumed, before I fled.

My father's only legacy, and I planned to down it.

AND THOUGH I AM SURE I made haste away from the house, and though it was a journey of several days, my father is still before me. It's not much consolation that my presence seems to make him as uncomfortable as his does me.

I have returned to my exile in Mr. Strick's pavilion, as far as I've ever traveled. My father is here in the pavilion, too. How can I sleep here now? There's barely any room. It was never meant to house me and all these brothers, and they haven't gone anywhere: they're still here, rattling in their empty jars in rows all around me, and now my father is with us, too, twisting over me, and other brothers are out there in the fields around us, and soon something dark will rise up out of Mr. Strick's pond. Not the moon, not the dawn, but a black dog, one big enough to pull me completely out of my cradle. My father will hitch a line to my hair, and then he will put on his headgear and walk all the way to the limits of his leash and beyond. There is a sound one cannot make except at the moment one is born into this deaf and mute world, a vegetal sound I didn't know I'd wanted to make but which my body has nevertheless been straining at for I don't know how long. I know no-one will answer it—it will fall on deaf ears—but I suspect that, like an echo, the sound is itself its answer, a kind of caring, a way of bringing hush.

Leson

Leson, it seems, is stuck even in his words and cannot think of another way to say it, so he repeats to this doctor the refrain his brain has lately taken up: I am stuck. Can you help? To which question what can a doctor answer? Maybe see a specialist? The unit's diagnostic program, confused by Leson's complaint, had sounded its chime and sent him here. Now this doctor was sending him elsewhere. No-one respects the gravity of my condition, Leson thinks. It is clear Leson will have to come up with a treatment of his own.

This doctor, though, is a professional. He has been trained to operate the appropriate diagnostic apparatuses. He affixes nodes to Leson, auscultates and palpitates and prods Leson. Leson plays along. He coughs, turns, coughs again. He keeps his head straight. He feels a tiny prick. The doctor tells him—though not in so many words—that what is wrong must be inside. Leson, he says, I know a good man. Here, in the colony. He recommends psychiatry. But it seems impossible to Leson that his fault could come from himself. When inert matter does not move, he thinks, no-one blames its lack of motivation. No-one claims the stone at the mouth of the cave is depressed when it refuses to roll away on its own. No, what Leson needs is a lever, a harness, a gantry, and so he describes his stuckness again, and then there is only silence in the examination room. Leson thinks of the other patients in other rooms. The doctor thinks of the same thing. Down the hall, a squeegeeing sound starts up. A very large woman is bleeding from her eyes, and a nurse, annoyed, is brushing back the tide with the sole of his shoe.

In the end, the only things Leson gets out of his visit are a bright blue blood pressure cuff, a pad of prescription forms, and a thin metal instrument he cannot identify but which has a pleasing smoothness in his hand. Though the latter two items had, at the time he'd taken them, suggested future uses, Leson cannot say why he has stolen the blood pressure cuff. Perhaps the color? It was not even the one the doctor had used on him. At home, he puts it on, adjusts it. The bladder inside inflates until it pushes against his arm, displacing the flesh around his blood vessels so that some essence of Leson rises to the surface to be measured and studied. Leson's arm tingles. He experiments with keeping the cuff inflated for longer and longer. There is a residual tingling in his arm. He puts the bulb down but leaves the cuff where it is. Perhaps, he thinks, he can inflate himself, squeezing the world around him until it reveals its answer. After such a prolonged absence of ideas, even this seems like a plan.

Such expansion, Leson thinks, would be, besides, strangely appropriate, as his dissatisfaction, the feeling of emptiness that preceded his dismissal from the service and the subsequent stuckness, had come from feeling no forward motion, no sense of progress, regress, or change. He could find no purpose. Now Leson would fill and move forward at once, and, best of all, he would avoid the need for any endogenous motivation. He had seen a frenzied zealousness driving men forward in the passage and on the front, but even though he had been engaged in the same work, he had never been able to find that same thing in himself. After a time his commanding officer, slowed no doubt by Leson's enervation, had finally summoned the disgust necessary to discharge him. There had been no warning—just, out of nowhere, a detail was dispatched to clean out Leson's bunk; idle hands, they'd been told. Soon after his dismissal, his family, too, had dissipated in the vacuum.

Leson, naturally, looked to his screen for answers. With more time to himself, he could take in yet more of this world, fill himself with its signals, and, with the help of the screen's perfectly simulated voices and textures, even perhaps become an expert on the human condition, a man of the world. Or at least, Leson thought, a man of the colony. Why not? A man of the world might not only be one who could move about that world freely and without fear; perhaps a man of the world could also become so by expanding *into* the world, a colony unto himself. But even after hours of continued exposure, Leson, saddened, instead felt only the same sense of stillness. He did not feel full, not even a little sated. The only colonists ever to appear onscreen were test subjects kept in crates in a conspicuously small section of the screen, illustrating the effects on the human body of various native remedies—the rest was all passage-worms, the front, the passage. Leson would have learned more from staying in the service. Leson, though, could take a hint. He wrote down the names of the tested substances, transferring the information to the prescription pad any time he heard *significant weight gain.* He was not so different from others, he thought. He could learn to accept help.

He presented these slips to the dispensary, and the dispensary in turn issued stapled bag after stapled bag, filling one plastic tub and then another. The man there warned Leson of the side effects and complications. A line formed behind Leson, and grew, and grew. Do not take these with these, or these with these, the man there said. Weight gain, the man there said. Impotence, the man there said. Suicidal ideation, the man there said. Leson could barely carry all the bags away.

Once he was home and had started his regimen of pills, suppositories, ointments, medicaments, and injections, it seemed to Leson that his time was better-spent—his sense of wellbeing had been thrown off even further, true, but he found that all the things onscreen, even those he'd seen before, held interest once again. He felt fuller. His sensations were once again sources of deep and abiding fascination to him. In fact, his raptness was such that he did not doze or sleep at all; without sleep, he did as much viewing as two Lesons. He may also have been speaking aloud to himself—shouting?—he could not tell. Every now and again, his neighbors complained. Leson! Knock that off! Leson! Leson, do you know what time it is? He would still himself, remain silent. Yes, Leson knew what time it was. His screen was set to the correct time, just like anyone else's. He had decided it was better not to respond for now. All of what he did at this early stage was only preparation, after all; before any outreach could begin, one should have reach, range. And so Leson would first have to grow. Silently, he took another pill.

LESON'S REGIMEN inflated himself around himself. In fitful daydreams, Leson imagined fibers twining around each other into wicks of muscle, calcifications of tissue, subduction zones under his skin rising in ridges. The growing pains, at times, were unbearable. There was fat, and there was muscle, and there must, underneath it all, also have been new bone. There were shelves of Leson, lobes, where once there had been only sheer cliff faces. He grew a tenth of an inch, in all directions, then another tenth, and another. The scale went around once, twice, and then continued, so that Leson had to do math in order to weigh himself. His waist expanded, sure, but so did his wrists, his fingers and toes, his neck, his ankles. All of his joints ached. He was losing shape, becoming blobular. Even if it had not been confiscated, he would no longer have been able to put on his jungle suit. His head did not fit in the bathroom mirror anymore.

THE SEAMS OF LESON'S COLONY SUIT split when he sat down, when he bent over, when he reached for something across the table. He could see through to his overstretched skin. Would it, too, split when it had reached the limits of its pliability? Leson set his index finger to one of the iridescent striations that had appeared on his left arm and, with his thumb and middle finger, brought together skin that once hadn't needed to be brought together, directing the unit's automatic first aid station to suture him where he held himself. He had some trouble extricating his index finger after.

The result was underwhelming, looking necrotic and empty to Leson, like the result of a brush with a miniature passage-worm. Leson thought to retrieve the instrument he'd taken from the doctor's office. Although this was not the use he'd foreseen for it, Leson could hold two opposing ideas in mind at once. He placed the needle end of the instrument against another of his striations, pinching the old skin back together and once again directing the automatic first aid station to suture him whole. Where his first pocket had been clumsy and loose, this new one seemed more like a pore opening onto the world. Permeability seemed a laudable goal to Leson then, something to which to aspire. He could afford, he thought, to let in more of the world, to grow through a kind of osmosis.

And so things continued with Leson, pocket by pocket. When the station had run out of binding, he considered how best to invite in the world. He settled upon stuffing his pockets with the grime that had accumulated near the baseboards and behind the furniture, all that now remained of his life before the stuckness. In time, these new catchments he had sewn into himself would foster new organisms, and this, Leson feared, would be uncomfortable, itchy and inflamed, but he thought of such discomforts as the cost of being in the world and he very badly wanted to pay his dues.

LESON PAUSED IN HIS LABOR, looking out of the greased window. A passage-worm slithered past, big as a unit, ganglia drifting in the atmosphere. Leson scratched at a hillock of himself and a pouch spilled open. Something inside drifted to the floor and scurried away. Men from the patrol passed, careful, paranoid. Leson thought of chipped concrete, of gravel, of sawdust. Slowly, he rubbed a dried eye. He had once been a stalk and now he was a pile. But a place must change to accommodate its inhabitants, Leson thought.

WHAT LESON ATE was made up mainly of powders and formulae, as it always had been, but, when it seemed he had reached his outermost boundaries without any resolution to his condition, he decided he'd have to branch out into the supposedly inedible flora of the colony. He worried about the things he would not be able to keep down, on their effects on his growth, but he knew something new was needed. Because these things had to be treated before human teeth could rend them, Leson stewed what he found in the cultures he'd cured in his pockets and pores. The resulting mixture disturbed the stuckness of his insides, it was true, but the effect was not freeing, not exactly. Still, Leson did continue to grow, through a kind of lasting, uncomfortable bloat. He felt, at times, like a termite mound. He could not supervise its comings and goings.

Time passed. On every passageway lever and disposal button, every wall and gate and trailing up the ramp of his unit, there were bits that had once been Leson, leavings, outpourings of his slow flood. He had thus found himself in an intractable dispute with the colony's health official and the unit's superintendent, both squeamish about entering his quarters, having been warned away from the unit by its fleeing former residents. There is something very bad happening there, they said. Very bad. People are falling ill, Leson, the super told Leson. They are being evacuated. Leson, slug-like, lolling and ecstatic with mood-altering substances and the shivering of another fever, smiled from his place on the carpet. These people brought with them some part of him wherever they went, and so yet another bit of him must have been freed. Open up in there, Leson! The colony health official is here with me. Instead, Leson inched forward, slowly barricading the door with his bulk. He felt as though about to burst. Leson! We'll have to get the patrol.

So now Leson's world has closed around him. Like his unit, his life has walls, a ceiling, a floor. He has not seen the star in months, has not breathed unrecirculated air. He has heard voices, but he is no longer sure they aren't his own. His thoughts trend in a single direction. Perhaps they always have.

And so Leson groans, having grown to perfectly meet his unit's measurements. It is almost a rumbling, this groan, the man has become so large. What it is not is a word. Outside, the superintendent has fallen ill, as has the colony's health official. All of the curious, in fact, all those who came to see Leson, are swelling. The unit's two remaining families—Leson's neighbors—disappeared in the night, and now there is no-one to hear his grief. Leson is alone in his enclosure. Who knows what has become of these neighbors? Somewhere, in some other colony, a medical center is dealing with something that does not yet have a name and which causes an unaccountable augmentation.

Meanwhile, at last, a patrol is mustered. The men arrive at the unit with their machines and immediately begin dismantling the structure. They do not know they are there because of a former serviceman. They do not know there is anyone at all inside. The front cannot wait for answers, so the patrol does not ask questions; while the unfasteners work, passage-worms cross the passage into the colony, and the jungle spills through the cordon with them. The first floor of Leson's unit is gutted and the parts are sorted and recommissioned, but one by one the patrol, too, falls ill. Soon their excavators and unfasteners and sterilizers stand idle next to the skeleton of the unit. The only walls that remain are Leson's, and, with the others ripped away, the murals of stains on those walls are all the more evident. From the outside, Leson's unit looks like a square of thin paper barely holding back some oleaginous substance. There is a noticeable convexity to the walls and the floor, even the ceiling. Those who pass by think it is probably best not to think about it.

Out on the streets of the colony Leson's former neighbors blimp, go lopsided like overripe fruit. No-one walks; some are rolled here and there, but it is arduous work, and the well become weary at it and then fall ill, too. The elements bear down, but only the largest shelters can be occupied. Rows upon rows of units stand empty. Passage-worms roam the streets, cleaning the bloated and occasionally boring holes through them with their ganglia.

A boy, seemingly abandoned by his guardians, looking like nothing so much as an immense, greatly-enlarged tongue, reposes in the square outside Leson's unit. His skin has transcended see-through; it looks instead as though turned inside-out and combed. Others might come along to help him—if there were others—but alone he cannot move himself, and so he has been there in the square for days. Rain has collected in the crevices of his body. Passage-worms swish past, taking away parts of the units to either side of the boy. A broken unfastener stands upside-down on the beaten dirt of the terrarium, and part of the low fence around the terrarium has come down. Something inside of this boy has collapsed, too, some important inner faculty. The sounds he is making would have embarrassed him before, when he was well, but they come out all the same. A moan, not words. In his bloodshot eyes, which roll back in his head and then return to focus somewhere above the plane on which other creatures still operate, one can just see his apprehension of the passage-worm opposite. He has never been this close to one.

The boy does not recall how he might have come to be here, or what he might have done to deserve this. Is he the superintendent's son? The health official's? Leson's? Who does he belong to? Did someone roll him here and then disappear, or did he himself make his way here before bloating? His limbs don't reach the ground; he could neither crawl nor claw his way anywhere now, so here he remains, for good or for ill. Is Leson's unit his home, behind him, on the square? Is that why he is here? The passage-worm halts, its ganglia flickering in the light. The moons have risen in the sky, but the star is still shining. Somewhere inside the boy's body, an enlarged organ is pushing aside some fraction of the faculties needed for continued functioning. Struggling, he takes a breath. Somewhere inside the boy, something is giving way. A stasis has been reached in the colony. It does not favor the colonists. The jungle's squid-like diaphanous bats descend, secrete their essences, extend their proboscises, and gently lift the boy up. He disappears into the twilight. A strange, chunky rain falls in his wake.

Perhaps disappointed, the passage-worm closes on Leson's enclosure. One by one, its ganglia press against the wall and wipe some part of it away, like jets of water playing on dusted glass. Leson, uncovered, weeps to see the world again—to see the trail of the boy leading upwards into the sky. Out flow his tears, and, along with them, the blood pressure cuff is finally delivered from inside the vastness he has become. The neighbors, the superintendent, the colony health official, the doctor, the patrol, the officer who'd discharged him: all of them and others slide out of Leson as manikins or manifestations of his grief. Their sloughed-off skins, like deflated balloons, drift lazily in the flood of jellied stuff pouring out of Leson and joining the boy's effluence. This sludge is violet, yellow, blue, red, and all the shades in-between, all colors at once, distributed across a spectrum or in an indefinable single band, depending on the angle from which one views it. This sludge is thick enough that the unfastener stands up in it, but magnetized, in motion, drawn onwards by the passage. The run-off makes its way across the colony, carrying the furnishings of Leson's unit and all the other things it picks up on its way.

As Leson empties and joins the boy in their combined current, but before he is finally spent, turned inside-out by the force of his expectoration—before, that is, what was once Leson floats on top of the last dregs of all he'd taken in, trickling along behind the rest on its way to the passage—perhaps Leson wonders if he has indeed been freed, or if his container has merely changed its shape to match his own. But then it is over and Leson's skin gets hung up on the terrarium's low fence and flaps under the last of the torrent, as though waving goodbye to it or else dismissing it.

The passage-worm, dragging itself just a bit too close to the former enclosure, accidentally impales this Lesonskin on its anterior ganglion. Without intending to, without even noticing, the worm rolls into the current and hoists aloft the last of Leson like a flag above its exostructure. Leson, what is left of him, flies for a moment before disintegrating simultaneously at every point touching the ganglion.

One imagines this scene as a scene of triumph. Leson isn't left to do so. Somewhere, though, something has finally moved. What is owed Leson?

The Before
Unapprehended

Somehow, though, this seems awfully familiar.

—

No, I'm not less bothered by his absence than you, brother. How could I be? We were eleven and now we are ten, and yet there is no body, none of us can name the one who's missing, and what must all that mean? This silence worries us equally. Or, no, not quite equally: I think we all now agree my verses were next. If anyone should want this lonesome rest to break, it's me. I mean, if I can't claim a deeper anguish at brother's disappearance, I can add to it the anxiety of not knowing what to say. The bodies of our departed brothers will only get heavier the more steps we take, and though we all share that burden, how many steps we all take under it—at least for the moment—is my responsibility. Glass houses, brother.

—

You make it sound so simple. I'm not prepared to... I've forgotten even my own verses now; I can't be expected to remember his! No-one's fooling anyone here, brother. You don't know them either. You would have spoken up earlier if you did. I might have been able to recite them if I'd known I was going to be called upon to do so, back when the last of you who spoke, spoke—*maybe*— but so many days later, I can't remember where whoever it is left off, much less what comes after that. Be reasonable. And, I mean, of course I remember parts of what I would have said—*of course*—but where that starts I can't remember, and so then everything else... This chapter, that chapter—does my tongue really have them in the right order? Which one comes first? Am I simply recalling things already recited? You know how it is. One uncertainty leads to another, and that one to another, and that one to yet another, until it's uncertainties all the way down. And anyway, the whole thing's moot: since whoever it is isn't here, I'd have to recite for him before beginning my verses, and I don't know his verses, and, clearly, no-one is going to step in to recite them for me, and so here we are, struck completely dumb. Still, this strange interruption in the ritual has given me a chance to think. What if this confusion, this silence, isn't such a bad thing? What if the ritual has changed, brothers? What if not speaking *is* his part, and this, what I'm saying now, is mine? Obviously the words aren't the same, and so the terrain they cover can't be, but perhaps the path they lay out for us will take us where we want to go anyway.

—

Yes, we're going a little ways off. I know! I've just said as much. You're an expert in the obvious, brother, a true master. But here is a fact that must have escaped you: like you, I've been following the verses and stepping where they tell me I ought to step. I'm carrying one brother now—I haven't shirked my responsibilities. But as soon as we hit this blear patch, I took on an extra load also—you see, even back then I felt certain the silence was in part my fault, but my mind drew a blank as to how to go about addressing the problem. We proceeded carefully through this impossible fog, not knowing that the brother who should have been reciting had already disappeared. Though there was no way to know our next step wouldn't carry us over the edge, my mind did not panic at the uncertainty of the path; instead, it mirrored the landscape. Empty. But *that* thought, that emptiness, panicked me, because I felt I was the cause of it and yet I couldn't think of how to remedy the situation. Even without knowing it, you'd all been waiting for me to speak, to reveal the path ahead. I know it; I had been, too! Yet nothing came. Look, you know my reputation. I'm not chary with my words, and last season, I carried three brothers up to the opening, but this—no thongs exist with which to hold up such a thing. I had come to believe I had to speak. I had to say *something*, even though I knew it would lead us off the path. What I had to say weren't verses, or weren't verses I could recognize, but while we are still alive we continue to move, and while we move the story goes on. That's how it's always been. So, even if what I'm saying now is clearly wrong, even if we're definitely not going in the right direction, at least this will be *something*. And you can see for yourselves I'm right—we find ourselves in unfamiliar terrain, sure, but at least it *is* terrain.

—

I agree. We probably ought to go back to the beginning. At least then we would know where we are. But the first verses escape me. I think I have them right in my mind, but when I try to speak them aloud my throat dries up and then my mind looses them from their tether. Every time! Let someone else speak them. No? Surely someone still remembers the beginning? I mean the very first verse? Not even the brother who recited it back when we started out this season? No? No-one. Then, please, let me speak awhile. If, somewhere along the way, any of you remembers that verse, let him recite it. Until then, bear with me. At worst, we'll keep climbing until someone remembers the words, and then we'll end up where we end up every season, at the opening, on the plain. A little the worse for wear, it's true, a little more exhausted, but so it goes. At best, we'll follow the one who's missing to some other place.

—

Yes! Think of it. Brothers, no matter what else you may say, no matter what the ritual tells you to think, you can't deny that the one who's missing is no longer on the path. Look for yourselves. Not a mote out of place. No errant brother anywhere along the Spire. For that to be the case, he would have had to—well, just listen. First, you must picture a hole in the Spire.

—

I know: there is none. You will have to use your imagination. This hole is very deep, falling down and away from the surface into blackness. Inside it, there is nothing. No light, no sound, nothing. You can't see through to the other side, and there seems to be no bottom. Although the brother who is reciting has stepped past it, and all ahead of you move forward as if nothing out of the ordinary can be seen, your eyes are drawn toward this man-sized void when the brother in front of you knocks a bone from its resting place and into the nothingness. You do not hear an impact. Startled, you slow down, look deeper into the hole, but the verses keep coming and so you must keep going forward or you will be lost, you will die from exposure, and your desiccated corpse will have to wait until next season to be carried up to the opening and thrown inside. Later, as you huddle with your brothers on the escarpment and think over your verses—which you will have to recite in the morning—the landscape you've already traversed will naturally become a blur. You have tomorrow's verses to recite, too much already to remember. If one wishes to revisit some earlier feature along the path, one begins the ritual again and comes again to the spot. It's arduous work and I don't blame you for not bothering. If someone asked you if you'd seen the hole the instant after you'd seen the hole, easy!—you'd say yes—but no-one asks you and so you don't think of it. And so it becomes a strange sort of sub-verse in the ritual, a verse half-written but then erased and written over, and then that rewritten verse is erased and written over again next season, and so on and so on. Most traversals have such sub-verses; we all feel that to be true, even if we cannot know it. Things we pass along our way briefly flicker at the edges of our consciousnesses—we are certain of them—and then they disappear. These things stamp themselves on our memories so imperfectly we can't recall them even if, later, we are questioned specifically about them. The ritual itself makes it so. Let's take my hole as an example. We passed it some time ago on our way up the Spire, notwithstanding the fact that we can look back down the Spire and see that it isn't there. Still, it's clear as day to me, even though I have to imagine the hole— that is, acknowledge it isn't real—to make it so. You see, I think our brother must have fallen into this hole, and if he's fallen into it, it must exist. But I don't remember such a hole, the same as I don't remember who it is who's gone. But then, that's the whole point of the hole, isn't it?

—

Look. If, later, back on the plain, on our way to the opening, I wanted to ask if you remembered this hole, I would first have to recite for you chapter and verse where it was I saw the hole, or where, at any rate, it is that I'm wondering if *you* saw the hole. That is, in order to ask you if you saw the hole and not be spouting nonsense, I'd also have to be asking where *in particular in the verses* you saw it; I could not ask you if you saw a hole nowhere— how could you answer? In first conceiving of asking you if you'd seen the hole, I would be asserting—to myself—that the hole exists, since I know you couldn't very well have seen a hole that didn't exist. But it goes without saying that, in forming my question into a string of words to be spoken, I'd also be covering over any memory of that hole, because of course in order to ask if you saw the hole where you saw the hole, I would have to give its presumed location via verses that do not already contain the hole, and so

I would, in asking you about this hole-where-a-hole-doesn't-exist, also thereby be asserting that no such hole exists. I couldn't very well ask about a hole in *the-path-is-level-and-unbroken-forty-steps-past-the-remains-of-our-brother-who-passed-away-from-the-woe*, could I? What could you say in response but *I think you must have the wrong verse, brother*? So the path, like the verses, closes over the hole, and the hole leaves the world without fully entering it. But then, to return to the original conception, of course there must be a hole, because how could I ask about it if there weren't? I mean a hole in theory, a hole in the language. And this is what I mean by sub-verses. There must be a reality that does not obtain, but does exist, and it seems to me that brother must have found it. What if he found a way to follow the steps given by these sub-verses instead of the steps the rest of us were taking, the steps given by the verses being recited? Where would such a path lead? Wouldn't it take him into regions that exist in the same way un-dreamt daydreams exist? Not *places*, exactly, but rather abstractions, premonitions, wherever it is things reside before they are conceived of. It would have to, wouldn't it? It would have to. That would explain his disappearance, his... non-existence. I can't think of another way to explain it, can you? Where does brother exist? Not in front of us. Not in any material space we can perceive. And yet we can talk about him, though we cannot locate him, not even by name—that is to say, in verse.

—

Look, we know a brother is missing. That much we know. What we do not know is where he is now or who he is. He is nowhere, nothing. Thinking this naturally puts me in mind of this hole, for how else can it be that our eyes can search the entire surface of the Spire and find not even a trace of him? He must have somehow fallen into the Spire. Of course; he cannot possibly have ascended from it! But then how can there be a hole that is not in any of the verses, a hole that is then not visible? You've seen for yourselves: no hole, no brother. And even more perplexing: how can it be that we do not know who it is who's missing? This further convinces me that I must be right. Like a feature of the Spire that briefly exists but is not recorded, it is *as though* the missing brother never existed. And yet of course we know that he must have once existed, because, again, we know he is missing, and what does not exist cannot go missing.

—

Sometimes I exasperate even myself, brother. I know, it is confusing. Possibly the whole thing's obtuse, or not well-suited to my purpose. Let's see. Take yesterday's gruel. At this moment, before I've asked my question—I'll get to it—that gruel was and is as pure as gruel ever is. In your memory, it is a solid and impregnable thing: gruel. Unadulterated. But what if I ask: wasn't there an emmet in your portion, an emmet you nevertheless didn't notice in your haste to get the stuff down? I mean no offense, brother, but even you can't deny it's inedible. Now, that emmet cannot be entirely dispensed with—it may be that it *was* in your gruel but you didn't notice it, and there is no way now to know which it is. Before I'd asked the question, no emmet. No question! After, emmet. Perhaps there were emmets in every portion. Perhaps there were more insidious contaminants—perhaps there were toxins, microbes, intoxicants, emetics. It's only now, now that I'm saying this, that any of it occurs to you, but now that it has occurred to you, it's impossible to completely deny. Why should your gut be rumbling so early in the day? Were your bowels loose this morning? Is the sinking of your stomach a response to the thought of what you might have eaten, or, instead, to what you really and truly did eat? The emmet has gone from inconceivable to imminently conceivable, transformed itself into a problem of perception and memory, which we know are reliably imperfect faculties. And the converse to all this must also be true: if we can manage not only to not talk of a thing—think of the emmet before I brought up the emmet—but also not to think of a thing, that thing will enter into some state of existence that is indeterminable. *Existence* seems like an inappropriate word for that state, but I don't know how else to put it. The emmet might have been in our gruel regardless of whether I ever questioned whether the emmet was there, and so, somehow, that emmet exists despite not being conceived of. What I'm saying is: our brother has made himself into an emmet-before-we-questioned-whether-there-was-an-emmet. We have ceased to be able to speak or think of him. I don't know how... Yes, brother?

So the waters and the earth were brought before the first father. He had been given the task of imparting to each thing a name, and the waters and the earth waited to see what they would be called, and a morning and an evening passed, and the first father gave them their names, waters, earth, and thus they were known. And the stars and the other heavenly bodies were brought before the first father, too, and the day and the night, and the first father named them also, and each star had to itself a name and forever after was known by that name. And the beasts of the field and the birds of the air and the creatures of the sea were brought before the first father, each one given a name, and thus the days and nights passed. The flowers in the Garden were likewise brought forth and named, and the trees, and the other growing things. And even the rocks upon the land, and the mountains that rose up out of it, and all the various features of the Garden—to each was given a name and by that name was known. And the first father looked around him, and it was good, and he saw that it was good, but for each name, for each new thing, there too had been created a step in a path, a path leading out of the Garden, and, because he had named all that had been brought before him and thus filled the Garden past filling, he had, with each name and each thing been displaced from where he began, at the center of the Garden, and thus he found himself far, far away from the center; far away, too, from that which had brought before him all of these things. And indeed, the first father found himself outside of the Garden and even so far away he could no longer see it or anything within it. And, too, he could no longer find the path that had brought him where he found himself, for it was not a path like those in the Garden he had named paths. This path was instead itself a name, and the last name, the one the first father had reserved for himself.

—

—

I, too, am sorry this season has come to such a frustrating close, brother. How could I not be? Still, I think we've come further than ever before. Certainly nothing to be ashamed of. Come, let's toss these old bones into the opening and rest our limbs.

Afterthought

I REMEMBER that at first I'd been impressed by his ideas and, even more, by the way he thought—what Calvino I think calls "lightness"—but then, after the introductory chapter was over, when Shklovsky put the abstractions aside and turned to his analysis of individual stories, my initial impression faded and I read through the rest of the book distracted, retaining nothing, putting it back on the shelf read but also, really, unread. When some time had passed and more customers had recommended his work to me, I forgot that earlier disappointment and read another one of his books, only to have the same sense of disappointment remind me of my previous disappointment. I think ultimately I read three of his books, though it's possible I read the same one more than once and didn't realize I was reading it again.

This, I should say, has been my reaction to almost all of the book-length literary theory and criticism I've ever read: that it is something exciting only at its conception, in its précis, its first pages, and when reading past those first pages, I'm reminded of the ideas I sometimes have just before falling asleep, of how I can almost never remember those ideas when I wake the following mornings, when, upon waking, I have only this vague feeling that, while I was asleep, I lost something unique and of great value, even though I also know, from past experience, that if I were actually to remember the idea I've forgotten, that idea would turn out to be something not worth losing sleep over.

I can't remember if it's Shklovsky's explanation or my own, but the essence of his idea, I think, is that all fiction, no matter how naturalistic it seems on its surface, is dependent upon a series of unlikely coincidences—the sword the disgraced footman uses to kill the hero in the duel that concludes the story turns out to be the same sword the hero's stepfather once forged, a sword that was stolen from the family smithy by the hero's biological father (not the man who raised him, in other words) at the beginning of the story—and the difference between a graceful writer and one lacking grace is that a graceful writer is like a skilled tailor (is the simile mine or Shklovsky's?) in choosing when to hide the coincidences or seams (and, it goes without saying, when to show them off) while the clumsy writer, the inexperienced tailor, can't help but reveal them, particularly when they most want or need to hide them. Because it confirms certain prejudices I have about how stories work, I think, maybe, if I'd had that idea just before finally falling asleep after once again washing my hands, smearing calamine lotion over my son's chest and legs, washing my hands, singing to him and combing his hair with my fingers until he fell asleep, then washing my hands again, brushing my teeth, and getting into bed, in the morning, I would have felt at least a little sad if I found I had forgotten it.

A story I read in the pediatrician's waiting room on Monday (I always bring a book even though my wife says it makes me look like I'm going to the beach or something, like I'm just there to get some reading done and not because our son has chicken pox and needs to see the doctor, even though really it's because someone once told me that the magazines in doctors' waiting rooms are right up there with the handles on toilets in gas stations as one of the germiest things in the world and because, in general, I don't have much reading time anymore, and this pediatrician almost always keeps us waiting fifteen or twenty minutes, even when, as was the case on Monday, we're the only patients there), the story 'Melina' by Lucia Berlin, brought the Shklovsky to mind.

In the story, the unnamed narrator takes her baby for a walk around her neighborhood in Albuquerque and meets a man she calls the Beatnik. She invites the Beatnik into her home and he tells her that a woman he was having an affair with in California, a woman named Melina, told him he had to leave the Bay Area because her husband was returning from a tour—the husband, like all the men in the story, is a musician. Melina, the Beatnik tells the narrator, is married and has just had a baby, but her husband is not the father of the child. The Beatnik is not the father, either, but, unlike the Beatnik, Melina's husband doesn't seem to know or want to know about Melina's many affairs, and this, I think, is the reason Melina has sent the Beatnik away.

The Beatnik tells the narrator all about Melina, everything he has learned about her life from Melina herself, and then he leaves and, in the story, it is many years later and the narrator has met a man and married him. She asks this man—who, she says, is quiet and not very forthcoming—to tell her about his first love, and so this man tells the narrator about a woman he once saw lying in the grass in a ditch, sunbathing, naked except for a pair of lace doilies covering her eyes (like the doilies that used to be served under ice cream, is what Berlin wrote, a strange detail I remember because it is strange), and with whom this man fell in love in an instant. Nothing could happen between them, though, because this woman, her husband tells the narrator, was the girlfriend of one of his friends, the friend he was living with at the time, who I think I remember was also his bandmate.

The story then skips ahead a few years. A woman named Melina comes to town with her boyfriend, a man who is friends with the narrator's husband. Of course this Melina is, as becomes clear after she and the narrator have talked, the same woman the

Beatnik told the narrator about years before. The narrator and Melina have a few things in common: they're about the same age, their partners are both musicians, and the narrator's child is the same age as Melina's. (And, although it is never made clear in the story, I think that actually the narrator and Melina have more than just those three things in common; the narrator either is much more like Melina than she admits or else wants to be much more like Melina than she admits. But when isn't that the case with narrators and the people they tell us their stories about?) The narrator reads Melina's palm and tells her what she sees in it: mostly things in Melina's past, although also some vague hints about her future, too. The narrator, as we know, is only telling Melina what the Beatnik has already told the narrator, but Melina, who doesn't know the narrator knows the Beatnik and thinks the narrator is a person she has only just met, is understandably awed by what she hears; I think I remember she calls the narrator a *witch*.

Later, after Melina leaves town, the narrator and her husband are lying in bed, talking—her husband, again, is the man who told her about seeing the woman in the grass and falling in love with her—and he says, That was her. Who? the narrator asks. The woman I saw sunbathing in the grass, in the ditch—it was Melina. That's where the story ends, or anyway it's the last thing I remember happening in the story.

To me, now—I mean just now, telling the story in summary like this—'Melina' seems like an obvious lie, a kind of wish fulfillment for the narrator or the author, and yet, even though I generally dislike the type of people who tell obvious lies, 'Melina' and stories like it are exactly the kinds of stories I most like to read. Somehow, I think, if the people who told obvious lies did not go around telling obvious lies but instead published those obvious lies as fictions, I might not be disgusted by them. On the contrary,

I might want them to tell me even more of their obvious lies. Instead of being disgusted by them, I might, I think, think of their stories late at night, while I'm lying awake, wondering how I would get along without my wife's salary, and thinking also, again, inevitably, about how much our son favors his mother and how few of my features he seems to have inherited and how, when he's heard what his mother wants to do for dinner or where she wants to go that weekend, he will always say that that is exactly the thing he wants to eat or the place he wants to go, too, even if—or maybe *especially* if—I've just said I'd rather do something else. I wonder if maybe this is why, so many years later, I still remember Shklovsky's idea, when, now, even thinking hard about it, I remember almost nothing else about the Shklovsky I read.

BEFORE OUR SON WAS BORN, my wife and I lived in different states for five months. It wasn't a separation, or at least that's what we told each other; no, it was simply something we needed to do for our jobs. She'd taken a position in another state, far away, because it was better than the one she had at the time, and because we both knew my job was coming to an end. Like her old job, her new job involved data tables and code and other things I'm sure I'll never understand (she accused me often of playing dumb, but even after she explained how to do it and had gone in and changed some settings on my phone, the phone refused to Skype with her, and the parts of my email address after the @ symbol were something my wife's new co-workers laughed about—a sign, they said, that I must be some sort of time traveler from the nineties), and, like her old job, her new job paid okay but still not quite enough to support us both, so I took her word that this new position was in fact better than the last and that things would turn out differently in this new place than they had where we already were. My contract wasn't up for another four months, when the semester ended, and my colleagues begged me to please stay and finish it out, everyone already had way too many students; sure, the state was short-sighted but think of us, think of the kids, and so I stayed.

Although we weren't together in the same city or even the same state, my wife and I talked on the phone almost every night during the time we were apart, and I flew out to our new city, twice, to help choose an apartment and to look for a job. For budgetary reasons, there was no school on Fridays, so, as my wife liked to tell me, I could have gone to see her more often during this period, but no, actually, I reminded her, we didn't have the money for that, even though I knew I probably could have gone at least one more time, and really what kept me from doing so was that I was tired and I liked the quiet of our increasingly empty apartment. She came back just once, to help me finish packing my books and the kitchen things I'd kept, and, of course, to visit me.

One night on the phone, when I very much wanted to go to sleep—we were, after all, in two different time zones on two different coasts—she told me a story about one of her new co-workers, a man named Boudreaux. She often did this, told me stories about people I had never met and who I would almost certainly never meet, people who, after she'd told me these stories, disappeared altogether from her conversation and whose names I'd stopped bothering to even try to retain, but this name was strange for the part of the country we were moving to, even though it was also a name that was very familiar to me, and so it stuck with me in a way the other names never did.

This Boudreaux, she said, wasn't outgoing but still he was nice, not unfriendly. He and his wife had two kids, a girl and a boy. The boy, she said, had health problems, because, she said, he'd been born two months premature. And this was weird: the son's name was the same as *my* name, both first and middle, though of course I'd never met this Boudreaux and his son had been born long before my wife had been hired to work with him. It was, in other words, a coincidence: caused, I felt sure, by the fact that both my first and middle names are somewhat common—not so common I'd ever met another person with both, but also not so uncommon I hadn't occasionally met people with one or the other.

The Boudreauxs' son, my wife told me, had been born very small, just shy of four pounds. He'd had serious breathing problems and had to have neonatal surgery to repair the curvature in his spine. Boudreaux brought the kid to work once: he spoke with a raspy, weak voice, my wife said, and was very skinny, but otherwise he seemed like a normal kid. Energetic, maybe a little hyper. Still, his parents had moved so far away from their hometowns and their families, in large part to be closer to the hospital and its specialists, the best in the nation, because of their son's many health issues, and they spent so much time at the hospital they each had their own favorite nurse and were on a first-name basis with all the billing people. This set of circumstances might have made me sad if I'd known Boudreaux or his wife, I thought, but, as it was, while my wife told me about the boy's conditions and allergies and all the things he could and couldn't do, I mostly just felt sleepy. Then she told me that there was something else interesting about Boudreaux—he was from a small town near where I'd grown up. Had I heard of it? Did I know him?

What I remembered best about growing up was driving around on weekends, smoking, drinking, and looking at sugarcane, rice, and more sugarcane. Although this period spans at most the two years that led up to me leaving for good, in my memory it has somehow come to represent all eighteen years I spent there. There was absolutely nothing to do anywhere within a forty-mile radius of my home town, and so I just drove until the tape I was listening to—a Columbia House ten-for-a-penny Dinosaur, Jr. or Public Enemy or Prince—popped out of the tape deck, end of

Side 1. Then I'd turn the tape over, take a different highway, and test the map in my head while I listened to Side 2. Most of the places I passed through on those drives were even smaller than my hometown: a church, a feed store or a gas station-and-grocery, maybe four or five big old houses on the main road, maybe a few side roads with trailers or smaller houses on them, and that was it. One of these towns was the one in which the girl I'd taken to my junior prom had lived, the town where I got my first speeding ticket, the same town where my wife was telling me Boudreaux had grown up. It was impossible that Boudreaux hadn't known the girl I'd gone to junior prom with, but this isn't a story in which Boudreaux was her brother or anything like that.

I think maybe I should say that, although I never thought of this girl I'd taken to junior prom as *my girlfriend*—things between us were never that serious—still, we did go out almost every weekend, for a period of, I think, six months, give or take. I didn't bring her home to meet my parents and she only introduced me to her father because he happened to be watering one time when I picked her up. But we made out a bunch and talked on the phone and I met most of her friends, including one in particular who came out with us a few times: a girl who, for all I know, might have been beautiful or smart or funny or all of those things, but what I remember about her now is that she had silky black hairs on her upper lip. That's terrible to say, I know, but it's what I remember. That, and that her last name had been Boudreaux.

We all hung out together a few times—me, my junior prom date, and her friend—squeezing in on the blue pleather bench seat in the little pick-up my parents let me drive, smoking cigarettes and drinking whatever we'd stolen from our parents' refrigerators or liquor cabinets, stopping off at the truck stop's twenty-four-hour restaurant for a late-night breakfast or cigarettes from the machine next to the bathrooms. And this girl, who I had completely forgotten twenty years later when my wife mentioned Boudreaux and his wife and their kid, this same girl, I eventually remembered, had a cousin about whom she'd once told me and my junior prom date, though, again, I didn't remember any of this when I talked to my wife that night—at most, during that phone call, there was my immediate recognition of the name of the town my wife mentioned and the complete and unsurprising familiarity of the name Boudreaux.

Because Boudreaux was a common name where I came from, the fact that my wife mentioned it in the context of that small town didn't signify much until the next day, when, packing another box of books, I remembered this girl and most of the story she'd told all those years ago. Boudreaux's wife had had preeclampsia, my wife told me. This had been a contributing factor in the baby being born premature. I remember I couldn't figure out why she was telling me any of this. (Now I think she probably told me those kinds of things because they related to something on her mind, like, if she was hungry, she might mention that someone she knew had just quit her job in data retention to open a soup and sandwich place, in the same way that I told her things, when I told her things, because they'd just occurred to me, for reasons that even I didn't always understand, at least not in the moment. Really, that's most of what I told her: things that didn't make a lot of sense when I said them out loud but which I felt, at the time and for reasons I didn't understand, were appropriate things to say, and I don't have a good reason to believe she was different from me in this regard.)

Eventually, that night, I said something to my wife that would embarrass me to repeat here—something about sex, in other words, because after all, by then we'd been apart a month, maybe longer—and that was, as I ought to have known it would be, the end of the phone call. I'm not saying I said something outrageous or perverted; no matter what I said, if it touched on sex, my wife would have reacted the same way, which was to tell me she had to go, she was hungry, it was dinnertime there, her brother was calling or she had to call her brother, something like that. Anyway, we hung up. I watched a movie on TV until I heard the neighbors' lock turning, then I went to bed. The next morning, taping up a box in the echoing living room, I remembered my junior prom date's friend's name.

SOMETIME AROUND JUNIOR PROM, sitting in that twenty-four-hour truck stop restaurant—I can still picture it perfectly, the vinyl clamshell booth in the corner, the cheap red runner that led from the front door past the PLEASE SEAT YOURSELF sign back to the waitress' station next to the smeared glass-lidded breakfast bar, and then, on the other side of a thin wood partition, the cigarette machine and the bathrooms—my junior prom date's friend, this girl who hadn't said more than ten words together any of the times she'd come out with us (I think I'd thought of her as a third wheel at the time, but later I wondered, thinking about the way my junior prom date danced with one of my friends' girlfriends at the prom, if maybe this friend hadn't been something more, or something else, whether after all *I* had been the third wheel), started telling us about her little cousin, a girl her brothers called Topher, as in Christopher, even though her name was Christine.

The girl told us that her cousin had been born with both sets of genitals, male and female. I know now this isn't really accurate, but that's what she'd said. The child's parents raised Christine as a girl, and the girl who was my junior prom date's friend said she'd always thought of Christine as a girl; she didn't find out about the whole two-sets-of-genitals thing until she was twelve or thirteen, when, she said, one of her brothers told her that their cousin Christine had been born a boy, and *he* was really named Christopher, not Christine, at which point, naturally, the girl who was my junior prom date's friend had gone to her mother, who told her that, yes, technically Christine had been named Christopher at birth, but there was much more to the situation than that, that wasn't the whole story, she wouldn't understand until she was older, and where had she heard all of this anyway? Then the mother punished the brother, who refused to tell my junior prom date's friend anything else about Christopher/Christine because she'd told on him, and so it had taken her a while to put together the rest of the story.

At the time, I'd thought she was telling us all this because that night—or was it the same night? the Friday before?—some guy in the truck stop had said something, loudly, about the hair on her upper lip when we passed his table on the way to our corner booth. I don't remember what exactly the guy said, but I do remember that it happened, mostly because I remember I'd laughed at whatever it was he'd said, out of a sense of wanting to feel like I wasn't the one being laughed at—he hadn't been impressed that I was laughing, I remember, probably didn't even acknowledge me—and then, afterwards and especially that night, I'd felt guilty about laughing, even ashamed, and, much later, the girl I'd taken to junior prom drank half a bottle of schnapps at some rich kid's boathouse after finals were over and told everyone within earshot (including me, though I don't think she knew that, but maybe she did) that I wasn't a very nice person. I remember thinking she couldn't possibly have known about anything I'd done that had been *not nice* except maybe for laughing that night at her friend, or, I guess, at her friend's expense.

(Now, though, I think the girl's decision to tell the story about her cousin Christine had nothing to do with the guy at the truck stop and instead came out of whatever had passed between my junior prom date and her friend when I wasn't around. I didn't see my junior prom date and this girl together after that night, which would, I think, have been shortly after junior prom, even though, before that, they'd pretty much always been together.)

That night in the twenty-four-hour restaurant, I remember, the girl told us that although her brother had been wrong—it wasn't that Christine was a boy when she was born but now was a girl—he'd also been right, sort of: the mother's ultrasounds had all shown that Christine was going to be a boy, and maybe the doctor didn't look close enough or it was just a time when doctors thought things like that didn't need to be explained to patients, but, regardless, everyone thought Christine was going to be a boy, and my junior prom date's friend's mother had even helped her sister-in-law—Christine's mother—paint the nursery light blue, with a border of baseball players or football players or something like that, and then, when Christine was born, the new parents hadn't known what to do.

The doctor wanted to operate—it seemed like maybe that had been the plan all along—and there were these pills he could prescribe to boost her testosterone levels or something, but then Christine's parents either weren't sure about the surgery or weren't sure about the doctor. Eventually they'd painted over the nursery's walls and officially changed the baby's name to Christine. They raised her as a girl. That the border with the baseball players or football players or whatever had shown through the paint was a detail I remember my junior prom date's friend made a point of mentioning.

When my wife told me this co-worker of hers was named Chris Boudreaux, the name didn't register right away. I knew the town she mentioned, but not this person. But the day after she told me the story about Boudreaux's son, I remembered my junior prom date, her friend, and her friend's cousin. Was the story that the cousin had been born a girl but raised a boy? I didn't think so. No, that wouldn't have made sense. After thinking about it for a few more days, I remembered that my junior prom date's friend had, when telling us all this, blurted out that her brother told her that their cousin had an *enormous clitoris*, and I think my junior prom date said that that made it sound like a rollercoaster or a daiquiri. It's strange what you remember. I thought there was no way this Boudreaux my wife had met was the same person I'd been told about but that maybe Chris was a family name or something, or maybe I'd misremembered the girl's name after all and gotten it mixed up with someone else I knew from back home. But then other things came up, more urgent things I had to attend to, and I didn't think any more about it, not for years.

WHEN THE SEMESTER ENDED I joined my wife in our new town, and we talked, again, about finally really settling down, maybe buying a house, having a kid. I think I said something to the effect of, Sure, maybe we can start trying, and then, of course, a week later, my wife texted me from work: *pick up your phone.*

I was happy about the news, but I'd also just lost my job and we were worried about how we'd make it through maternity leave, to say nothing of what would come after. The local school district had just announced their own layoffs, so I applied to every job I saw with an opening, and that's how I ended up working for the bookstore, making next to nothing but just enough to get us through.

People think that working in a bookstore must be great: you get to read all the time and talk to people about books. How bad could it be? Really, though, it's a retail job, meaning you're on your feet all day and most of the people you talk to don't know anything about books and if the manager catches you reading on the job, you get written up, just like anywhere else. Still, I liked it for how quiet it was most of the time, and how little it asked of me other than a certain amount of patience and the ability to ignore the near-constant micro-managing of each new supervisor. My wife and I talked about the job being transitional, something to do until I found another teaching position, but then I never did transition to anything else and I stopped bothering to pretend I was trying. Our son was born and then my wife got a promotion, not too long after she'd returned to work, and even though during her leave I'd been training to become a shift manager, afterwards, instead, I dropped down to part-time, nights only, so that I could be home with our son during the day.

There was, by then, really no reason for me to keep the job at the bookstore, but I liked getting out of the house even though it meant I only got to see my wife a few nights a week. The job was, in its way, relaxing; there were few customers and even fewer demands, and I could usually get through my shifts without ever having to have a conversation that went beyond small talk. The only real challenge, as in all the jobs I've ever had, was getting along with the people I worked with. Fortunately, because the pay was so bad and the company tried its hardest to avoid giving anyone benefits, there was a lot of turnover, which meant that if the new cashier wouldn't stop talking about his black metal band or the new shelver blabbed on and on about the fantasy trilogy she was writing but hadn't started *writing* writing yet or the new info desk guy kept recommending *The Fountainhead* to kids, at least you knew they probably wouldn't be there very long.

One day one of the new cashiers, a high schooler with interesting hair who told me she liked my name, came up to the info desk, told me I wasn't doing anything, and asked me to shelve the literature section for her. Not: *do you know where the stuff in this lug goes?* but: *put the books in this lug where they go.* She held up her phone as if to show me something—it was on the lock-screen, a picture of a cat—and explained she was having a hard day and was going out to the loading dock, so, if the manager asked, she was in the bathroom or whatever and would I whistle or knock or something if it looked like anyone was going out the back. It didn't seem like the most thought-out plan. I think I admired her shamelessness, but, even so, I didn't shelve the books for her. She got written up for taking an unauthorized break and, after that, you could tell, she had a grudge against me.

The kid who kept trying to get his street name, Toast, put on his name tag, but whose name tag instead said BRAIN—his real name was Brian, but the store manager disliked him and pretended to be dyslexic, and told Toast it would be a while before the whole thing could get sorted out, and Toast said he preferred BRAIN if he couldn't get TOAST anyway, and so, even after three months, his name tag still said BRAIN—told me that this girl, the new cashier, had found out her dad wasn't her real dad the day she got written up, and had been kind of freaking out about it. She didn't show up for her next two shifts, and, as desperate as the manager tended to be to not have to go through the trouble of hiring yet another new person, still, normally, she would have been fired when, on the third day, she showed up on time only to leave an hour into her shift after screaming at a customer (and, I'm pretty sure, after throwing out my Thai food, a massaman curry I'd put in the breakroom fridge), but the manager was on vacation in Honolulu that week and so no-one there *could* fire her. Somehow, probably because everyone else was at least fifteen years younger than me and because I had been at the store longer than any of them, the night manager asked me to talk to her when she came in for her next shift. He said he'd give me a full hour for lunch that day, so I didn't complain too much.

It's just that he was a total hypocrite, she said. He'd told her he wanted her to understand it wasn't easy, as though she didn't already know that, as if her life had been easy, as if *she* had it *easy*.

She wasn't looking at me. She asked me if the night manager was going to clock her in or if she needed to do it. She had black nails with a cartoon ghost painted in the middle of them, I remember. Although, before, she'd told Toast that she'd known all along, that it was obvious and didn't need explaining, he told me she told him that her father had never actually come out and said anything about his childhood (he'd been bullied at school, her mother told her, and sexually assaulted, and his parents were *of a different time*), not until her mother found her chest binder and, during his weekend with her, her dad had tried to talk to her about it, about their family. She wasn't saying he wasn't her dad, it wasn't like that, *she* wasn't like that, but things were just different now, you know? How could they not be? He hated to think of *how she could be hurt*, she said he said. He *knew what she was going through* and *supported her decision*, she said. He didn't know anything, she said. He was assuming, like he always did, she said.

I'd only ever known her first name; like everyone else, she'd had a name tag. She'd worn it her first week and then never again. Of course there were those HELLO, MY NAME IS stickers behind the info desk for people who'd lost their name tags, but I never saw her wearing one and guessed she got away with it because the assistant manager was looking for a better reason to fire her and was sick of arguing about it every shift. Toast told me she went by Beck, though that wasn't the name I remembered from her name tag—Mona, a name I don't think I'd ever forget. I'd only ever known most of my co-workers' first names; there was no reason for me to know their last names. I didn't go with them after work to the theme restaurant bar next door, I didn't know when their birthdays were or whether they lived alone or had spouses or partners or roommates. Still, without even thinking about it, I asked the new cashier whether her father's name was Chris and whether her last name was Boudreaux. At first she looked surprised, then she told me I wasn't the manager, it didn't matter that I acted like I was the manager, I wasn't the manager, I was nobody, I was just a weird old loser, and then she asked me if I knew how pathetic everyone thought I was, and, after that, I never saw her again.

I'M PRETTY SURE it was Lakoff who pointed out that the idea of plot, the way we typically use the word, is a metaphor, though it seems possible the observation doesn't come from him. We say that stories have plots, strings of incidents brought together by coincidence and selective memory, but we don't usually reflect on what it is we're saying when we do. These things in stories we call plots are related, at a deep level, not only to the kinds of plots that are schemes to commit crimes but also to the kinds of plots that are parcels of land. A story with a plot, then, couldn't have *a point*—a single one—any more than a farmer's field could consist of a single point. Think about plotting the points on a graph that define a triangle, a rectangle, a square, or all the points that fall inside their boundaries. To talk about a story having *a* point would seem to imply that it doesn't have a plot, since a plot is a field made up of many points. A single point is only ever just that: a single point.

My wife used to get angry and complain that I was talking to her the way, she said, a teacher talks to their students, explaining things that didn't need to be explained, at least not to her, even when it was obvious they were things we each had very different ideas about. Really, though, in general, I don't like to explain things, don't even like talking all that much, possibly as a consequence of having spent so much time teaching high schoolers. I've never been able to make myself believe that talking accomplishes anything. When the new cashier said what she said, I didn't answer. I didn't tell her that, yes, I knew how pathetic she thought I was, or that I knew she wasn't the only one who thought I was pathetic (the manager also thought this, I knew; and Toast, who once told me he lived part of the week in his girlfriend's squat, had seemed surprised the first time the sitter brought my son to the store—surprised, I mean, that I had a family—and afterwards he treated me like I had brain damage or a weird smell), and, later, when the night manager started his shift, he asked me what had happened and I said the new cashier told me she wasn't coming back and that was really all I knew.

I'VE JUST REALIZED why the title 'Melina' seems so familiar to me. Once, long ago, maybe in my first year at the store, I read a used copy of *Malina*, the novel by Ingeborg Bachmann. The Malina in that book is a man, not a woman, and, from what I can remember, the book is really about the narrator, not Malina but a woman who lives with Malina. I can just barely remember being confused about the title of the book, because it is fairly long and Malina doesn't actually appear until halfway through or maybe even further on. He's mentioned once or twice in the first few pages, but then most of the first half of the book, nearly all of it, is about some other man, and then there is, I think I remember, a section about the narrator's father—maybe there's incest? some sort of abuse, I think—and then, in the third of the three sections, Malina finally appears, although, even then, he doesn't really do anything. The narrator lives with Malina, but the two don't interact, not meaningfully. In fact I don't think it's ever made clear what type of relationship the narrator and Malina have—I have an impression that the narrator hides her relationship with the other man from Malina, but at the same time I also have an impression that Malina and the narrator don't share a particularly intimate relationship, not one that would seem to require that the narrator hide an affair from Malina.

In fact, by now, I've forgotten so much about *Malina* that the only part of it I remember with any clarity is the very end, when, I think, the narrator somehow disappears as though shrinking into nothing. Because she's still narrating, it can't be that she's dead, but there is, I remember, something about murder, and, in what I recall being my favorite passage in the book, a description of the things of the narrator's that Malina cleans up or throws out, until finally there is nothing of hers left in the apartment.

Until that part, the very end, I think I'd been sort of ambivalent about the book; I can remember a friend of mine telling me I *had* to read it, and then, when I read it, I wasn't sure I was going to finish it, and I probably only finished it because I worried my friend would ask me what I'd thought, and because it had been difficult to find a copy and I'd have felt ashamed if I didn't finish it. I'm not sure what it was about the book that made me so ambivalent, but I do remember feeling like the ending made up, a little, for the fact that I'd stuck with it, although I'm not really sure why that is. I mean that it seems strange to think an ending where the narrator and her story just kind of slip away into nothing would be satisfying, much less make up for feeling ambivalent about the hundreds of pages I'd read to get to that point. I've sometimes wondered why it is that I'm able to remember I loved something or hated it, but not able to remember what specifically I loved or hated about it, how I came to form the opinion I have.

The stuff about my son and his chicken pox is true, by the way, and I'm sure about the Shklovsky, the Berlin, the Lakoff, and even, to the extent that I remember it at all, the Bachmann. There are things, I mean, in this story that are exactly as I've put them down. But other things are more complicated. For instance, the Boudreauxs, my junior prom date's friend, and most of the stuff about my wife. There are, I've discovered, periods of my life that I'm not able to shake loose, even many years after the fact, periods when all the details, including the most mundane, seem to remain instantly accessible forever, though I've also learned that that degree of certainty can be deceptive. The brain, I have come to understand, has this inscrutable way of ruffling our pasts so that the crests and valleys of events somehow come to rest at the same distance from true. The trouble is that we find lies seductive, even when, or maybe most especially when, they are most treacherous to us.

I guess that's all I can really say for sure: that there are things in my past I'm sure of but that, for reasons I don't understand, those things seem to be few in number and in any case my certainty is suspicious to me. Of course I remember the first time my son asked about this person his mother had brought home. We'd been sleeping in different rooms for a while by then, my wife and I. What my son said about this person was confusing, so confusing I didn't feel sure that what he was saying wasn't something he'd dreamed up, and I'd taken it seriously only because it matched what I felt the situation could have been. I mean that it confirmed some suspicions I'd had for a long time.

Although it was very early in the morning, and earlier still where they were, I called my parents—what else could I do? My mother answered. She's always been an early riser. She told me that it isn't true that I haven't had a good life, but I hadn't said anything to the contrary at that point in the conversation. I asked her what she'd been thinking about, why she'd said that to me, as though there could be an answer to a question like that. She asked me if my son was there. She told me to put my son on the phone. She wanted to know what he wanted for his birthday. How old was he going to be? I heard her ask him. I heard him say a number I knew was not right; he was already that age, he would be a year older on his birthday. I am not sure my mother knew; she didn't correct him. When he told her goodbye, I reached out to take the phone back from him, but, by the time I said Mom? she'd already hung up.

Babel

A STUDENT NEAR THE AISLE in the middle of the auditorium stood up and walked out just then, looking down at the phone in his hand, and, at that instant and apparently in reverence, the little man paused in his speech and lowered his gaze. He said nothing. In that moment, in that silence, the little man wondered whether he had, finally, strayed too far from the course's designated topic. Although he then tried to resume speaking, the little man found he couldn't recall what he'd been planning to say next. Something about the building of the Tower of Babel, he thought. Yes, it seemed likely, in that instant, that the foundations laid for the Tower of Babel had been the subject of the sentence he'd started and then abandoned, but when he looked down at his lecture notes he could not find the words "Tower" or "Babel" written anywhere in them.

In another story, all this might have been only a dream. We are perfectly familiar, after all, with the implications of such nightmares. We have had them ourselves. In such a story, our little man would have awakened, perhaps long before dawn, perhaps unable to return to sleep, and, despite himself, he would have enacted, in his waking decisions, the anxieties of the night. The thing he truly feared, the thing for which this dream had been nothing more than an unbearably pregnant symbol, would come to pass, and he would be unable to face it, and he would then think of this dream.

Or perhaps he would instead have forgotten it. Perhaps, in yet another variation of the story, the dream, mentioned at the beginning of the story, in passing—the little man waking in a cold sweat; was it something he ate? was it stress?—would not seem so remarkable to the little man, and even for us, the readers, would come to have significance only on the very last page. There, the little man's elderly and infirm father or mother, or perhaps someone else close to him, would, after some disappointment or disagreement, walk out on him, as we would understand it, forever, and the little man would once again lower his gaze, finding himself speechless and powerless to act. He isn't going to try to stop them? He isn't going to say anything? Eventually, perhaps, it will occur to us that we have been given our answers already.

And if our story is one in which the scene in the auditorium represents waking life and not a dream, then perhaps in that moment the little man would have cleared his throat, polished his glasses, or else remained still, storing up the quiet around him. Maybe, the little man in this other story would think, it had been an emergency, maybe someone had called to tell the student his father was in hospital or his brother or sister had passed away. The student hadn't seemed panicked, but perhaps, the little man would think, his blank face had been a kind of mirage, the effect of the distance between them.

This story, though, the one we are reading, does not make the choice to follow the little man through time. Although in its refusal it risks losing us, releasing us from its still-tenuous hold, this story leaves the little man at the podium to pull into a parking spot on a one-way street. It is the little man's least favorite spot, too close to the hydrant and half in a pothole. In this story, at this moment, we do not know why we have landed here or what it has to do with what we've read so far. All we know is that, when the little man emerges, the elephant ears that were bent against the Honda brush against his side, and then, following that fleeting contact, in the neighbor's porch light, the little man checks and rechecks his pants and his jacket for insects. Because he is so consumed with this—is his fidgeting the result of some horrific past experience or is it only that he has imagined things crawling on him, unseen?—and because the city in which the little man lives, having more pressing budgetary concerns after the storm, no longer seems interested in keeping its streets lit, the little man does not see the other man step from the shadows. The little man, shaking the sleeve of his jacket to dislodge something—is it something?—does not see the gun.

Robert, this other man says, though the little man's name is not Robert, we have to talk.

All right, the little man says. Let's go inside. It feels like it's going to come down.

The little man, we understand, means rain.

So now, in this story, there is a gun. In another story, the man with the gun would be the little man's student, perhaps the very student who got up and walked out on page one. Is it that the shorter the story, the farther the reader's credulity must be stretched? There is no answer in our story. Indeed, our story sets aside both the gun and the identity of the person wielding it and now tells us that, as a child, the little man had been treated differently from other children. He had, we are assured, seldom asked for it, though of course we know he could not avoid asking for it at times. We all need help. He had been treated kindly, softly, as though fragile, and all of this delicate handling had intensified his sense of isolation. In reaction, he had attempted a kind of invisibility, but this had somehow only improved his charm. Our story chooses one example from among many in the little man's past: a minor transgression, a neighbor whipped or a schoolmate suspended, the little man unpunished. He will not have asked for this indirect forgiveness, but he will be granted it. The whole thing is summarized and thus made general through its attempted metonymy. That it happened is unexceptional, the story seems to say to us; this is not the story of that tragedy.

So surely, we think, we'll now return to the matter of the gun. It's fine to give us background on our characters—we expect it, even in the shortest of stories—but if meanwhile we're distracted by thoughts of their present, we become quite impatient. After all, if we see a stranger mugged on the street, we help her or we don't, but we don't typically stop to wonder whether she lost a parent as a child, whether she herself has lost a child, whether she's been abused or bullied or has been to war. And perhaps, we think, it's important to care about the little man more than that stranger—the stranger is real, palpable; her problems are naked before us and within our power to affect—and, only a few pages in, we can't summon that kind of pathos yet, not for the little man. But then, telling us what the story has told us of the little man's past hasn't done much to develop him, and anyway ours is a very simple curiosity: what is happening? Maybe the other man *ought* to be the little man's student, we think. Maybe the test of the reader's disbelief would be worth it if it meant a more satisfying shape to the story.

Another story, reducing things to their barest essence, might zoom in on the scene of the little man and the man with the gun, together now in the little man's living room, giving each gesture, each tiny action, an outsized significance. The way the other man handles the gun would become an indication of his character— careless, on his lap, unhandled? aggressive, in his hand, pointing? nervous, held close to the body to prevent shaking?—and thus it would tell us as much as we need to know about him and his relationship to the little man. We may decide, reading into his actions, that this is a mugging, but we may instead decide that it is only a long-running disagreement, or else possibly just a tragic misunderstanding.

Our story, though, does not reduce. It continues to sprawl. In not focusing on this scene in the living room, in moving through the backstory and then throwing us into a future moment, our story is indicating that the scene in the living room is, like the whipping or the suspension, really only one incident in a much longer history. An example, yes, but *one* example, not the only or even the best, just the one that leads the little man, finally, to call the police and tell them about this strange relationship he and the other man have had for nearly two decades. And when the police have apprehended the other man and he is on trial, our story might give us details of the trial or even some facts about the case, but instead our story allows these things to remain implied.

In fact, our story is, generally speaking, short on explanation and careless with details. Another story would certainly have gone out of its way to explain why the other man called the little man Robert. That detail is far too interesting to simply throw away. In such a story, we would have a scene with the little man in a different car, a much larger and fancier car, a luxury sedan perhaps, accidentally side-swiping a parked Buick in a neighborhood he'd never been to before. In that story, a man will then jump into the passenger seat and tell the little man to drive, to just go. This will be our other man. The little man in that story will at first think he is being carjacked—it is, in that story, in that scene, the 1980s, a time when, we all know, things like that happened—but this other man will explain that, after all, he is saving the little man's life. The car the little man has hit in this other story will be this other man's uncle's Buick, and this uncle will be the boss of the neighborhood, and the men the little man in this other story has seen on the corner will beat the little man if he is fool enough to stick around, or so our other man will tell him. In this other story, the only thing to do—because police don't come to this neighborhood to help and nobody there has insurance—will be for the other man to take the money for the repairs to his uncle. The little man in this story won't have the money on him, and so the little man will, reluctantly, have to give the other man his address. And so, in this other story, it will start.

That we aren't given this sort of information, this backstory—how does this change how we see things in our story? How much do we miss a scene in which the other man goes to the little man's house with an estimate written on what looks like the back of a grocery bag? We might feel, when the little man brings out the envelope with the bank logo on it, that we've come to know something more about the little man, about his innocence or perhaps instead about the extent of his guilt. In such a scene, in dialogue, we might also learn that, although the little man has given this other man his address and quite a bit of cash, he hasn't given him his name—that, for the little man, words matter more, somehow.

Our story has none of this, but because it doesn't, it is freed of the responsibility of showing us what a weak protection such behavior would be: freed, that is, from giving us yet more exposition in the form of the little man's thoughts when, years later, after the little man has paid the other man again and again—because, well, times are tough after the hurricane and the other man doesn't have any work and his children are going hungry—the two men once again find themselves on the little man's back porch, the other man sweating heavily through a dark shirt, jittery, and the little man, on summer break, conscious that he is, at that very moment, being paid for what sometimes seems to others nothing at all, things like reading the same page of the Bible over and over, thinking about the different ways the different translators have rendered this one passage and then, after a day at the university library or his office, relaxing in his backyard, watering tomatoes that will be eaten by insects long before they've ripened, his mind turning not to the classes he'll teach but instead to these children he's never seen, children he can't be certain actually exist, but who, in his mind, are going hungry because of a mistake he made long, long before, and so, really, did it *matter* that the little man didn't believe the other man's stories? Somehow he felt that his own lie, the matter of this fake name, was worse. Is our story aiming for concision in keeping such a scene from us, or is it merely being withholding?

Many versions of this story, including ours, will at least have a scene of the little man in the courtroom, at the plaintiff's table, the bailiff reading the little man's name—not Robert but his real name—and the other man leaning back in his chair and giving the little man a look that will at least partly explain why, midway through the trial, after he himself has testified that this other man *did* point a gun at him in his own living room, *did* demand money, the little man will nonetheless be amazed that the state has charged the other man not only with armed robbery but also with kidnapping, and he, the little man, will think, These lawyers aren't doing much to prove this man threatened me or took my money by force, much less kidnapped me. It's my word against his. If he were a man like me, the little man in such stories will think, he could not be convicted, not on this evidence. I invited him in.

Which is not to say that the little man is so naïve as not to expect that the jury will convict the other man, and when, in all versions of this story, they do, he does not feel vindicated. In our story, this is when the look the other man gives the little man is described—in a flashback, a single sentence—and then immediately we jump back to the end of the trial and our little man walking out of the courtroom, regretting calling the police in the first place, thinking about the other man's family and the looks they, too, had given him.

Our story, restless as ever, will then tell us that, at some point during the decades of his extortion, the little man had stopped lecturing on his subject of expertise, stopped talking about it almost altogether. Instead, in our story, he will create what he will think of, simply, as stories—perhaps instructive, perhaps not—delivering them instead of his lectures. In our story, the chair will interview the little man's students, the little man's colleagues. The little man's colleagues will think he is simply testing the limits of tenure. They will plot ways to get back at him—though for what, exactly, they will never be able to agree on. His students, it turns out, will be just as puzzled as his colleagues, though they will pass on word that there are few assignments in his classes, that all you have to do is show up and listen to this little guy tell weird stories about the world and history and then summarize those things in your papers and you'll pass.

In our story, things will go on in this way. We will wonder whether this has been the thrust of the story all along. The little man will no longer imagine his life headed in any other direction. Everyone in our story will accept that this has always been his fate. They will not, in other words, wonder that he is alone, that he is seemingly permanently stalled in his position, that he is never seen at social functions, that he may have intended something quite different for himself. He will have become, to them, a fact of life, not quite invisible but also not worth thinking about. Perhaps in another story all this would be given a scene, but our story, we know, resists this kind of narrative strategy. At what point will we finally lose patience?

Our story, teasing us, now gives us the tiniest hint of one of the little man's story-lectures. Finally, some bit of detail. Are we back at the beginning? The little man is at the podium, and now we have actual reported speech, words that we think have come from the little man's mouth: While it is common to think of the Tower of Babel as an aspiring to Godhood on the part of man, it isn't always presented that way, the little man says. Though its builders do intend that the Tower reach the heavens, they don't always seem to mean for it to rival the heavens, the little man says. After all, a finger pointing at the stars does nothing to approximate those stars. The Tower is, in some translations, little more than a beacon or a landmark, a tether for the men of the world, a place to congregate, like the temples of the Mayans or the mounds of the Native Americans. It is only the God of some translations of the story that introduces the element of hubris, of rivalry. What if we instead imagine that this interpretation is a mark of the cowardice of the writer or writers witnessing the destruction? the little man asks. What if we instead see the destruction as merely the natural result of some inescapable design flaw, a structural defect, the way we'd see it today? Instead of a jealous god, just a basic and all-pervasive incompetence; instead of a pernicious scrambling of the mother tongue, a beneficent screen drawn ever so slowly between peoples?

In this story, his students will write, as his previous students have written, the things he has said in his story-lecture. They will not cite him as a source, nor will they transform what he's said or take issue with it. They will simply present it to him as though it were their own, and in this way remind him of the fragility of knowledge, of the frangibility of fact. When he passes away at the end of our story, his teachings, such as they are, will live on under other names, smuggled into consciousness every now and again like mental contraband, perhaps even then completely inscrutable to those in possession of them.

In this story, the police will break down the little man's door after a neighbor complains of the smell. They will find long lists of money paid to the other man—itemized amounts, followed by short descriptions of the reason for the payouts—written on the backs of student papers. They will shake their heads at the gullibility thus displayed. Some people, they will say. They will say that the little man could have retired early on this money, could have gone on dozens of expensive vacations, could have bought a better house in the city and a camp on Lake Borgne or Grand Isle. What they would have done with it! When added up, it will be more or less incomprehensible to those doing the adding that the little man didn't turn in this other man much sooner; that, after the other man got out of jail and resumed this strange relationship, the little man didn't turn him in yet again; and that, in fact, inexplicably, the little man instead started giving him even more money. One of the investigators will make a joke about Big Brothers, Big Sisters.

These police will also, of course, find the little man on the kitchen floor. He will have been dead for several days. In another story, there will be a gunshot wound in his body, because the gun, having been introduced, ought to go off, but in our story, the little man will have died peacefully. Another detail discarded. In another story, his papers will say something profound, something about his life, his conflicted charity, but in ours, there will be no papers, not written by the little man. There will be only the papers of his students, and, on the backs of these papers, the little man's accounts.

At the top of the most recent stack, a date from two weeks before, an amount in the hundreds, and the words *sister, dialysis*. On the other side of this paper, one of the little man's students will remind us that the Tower was not built in Babel but in Shinar; that, after the destruction of the Tower, the city was renamed Babel; that this is a pun, because, in Hebrew as in English, the word

Babel resembles the word *babble*, which is to say, a confusion of sound, an almost-nonsense that nevertheless indicates that another person, a beating heart and a mind at work, is close by, some human being within earshot who we nevertheless find we cannot understand.

Acknowledgements

'(   ),' 'The Invention of an Island,' '*La tortue* or *The Tortoise*,' 'Leson,' 'The Before Unapprehended,' and 'Babel' were all first published in *Conjunctions*. Bradford Morrow's encouragement and guidance were instrumental in each case. 'Fathers and Sons' and 'A Field in Winter' first appeared in *Vestiges*, whose editor, Jared Daniel Fagen, made both of them better.

Thanks are due Brandon Hobson, Susan Daitch, and Ben Loory for their kind words and generosity.

This book would have taken a very different form if not for the tireless work of its editor, Daniel Davis Wood.

SPLICE
ThisisSplice.co.uk